BLOOD TRAIL

A JOHN JORDAN MYSTERY, BOOK 18

MICHAEL LISTER

PULPWOOD PRESS

ISBN: 978-1-947606-10-4

Edited by Aaron Bearden

Design by Tim Flanagan

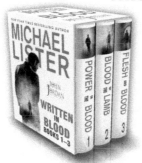
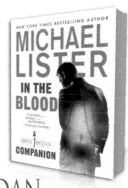

For Tony Simmons

a gifted wordsmith, an insightful artist, a person of great integrity.

I'm honored to call you friend. I'm grateful to have been able to do so for so long.

BLOOD TRAIL

1

"Who was that?" Anna whispers.

Her voice has that sweet, sleepy quality that is irresistibly soft and sexy.

I replace the phone on the bedside table and turn back toward her. "Reggie," I say.

She glances at the red numbers on the ceiling—the time of 3:43 A.M. being projected from the clock on her bedside table.

Our bedroom is dim, the only illumination coming from the blood-red digital readout on the ceiling and the small nightlight inside the master bath.

The room is cool and breezy, the constant swirl of cold air coming from a window unit and box fan, which we run all night, every night, even though we have central air conditioning. We both sleep better when our bedroom is just this side of arctic.

Because of the unhinged and threatening actions of Chris Taunton, Anna's ex, and my own personal trauma of recently working a child murder case, we have moved our girls' beds into our room—Taylor's baby bed and Johanna's big girl bed, which they are sound asleep in now.

"What is it?" she asks.

"Chris," I say. "He's dead. Been murdered."

Chris is not only Anna's ex but also Taylor's father.

I reach over and put my hand on her shoulder not because I think she needs comfort, but because she might need support. It's shocking, if not completely unsurprising or unwelcome news.

She doesn't say anything.

"You okay?"

"I'm not sure how to feel about it," she says. "I assumed I'd feel nothing . . . but . . . I don't know. It's strange. I do feel something. Just not sure what it is."

I caress her arm beneath the covers.

"It's a jolt," I say, though I'm not sure it is. She doesn't seem particularly surprised. "There's no right or wrong way to feel about it. Feel what you feel without judging yourself or asking what you're supposed to feel."

She nods. "Thanks. Part of what I feel is relief."

"Of course," I say.

Not only had Chris tried to have Anna and I killed, he had been stalking us for months, and had recently broken into our home with a gun and taken Anna and the girls hostage.

"It's like . . . like waking from a bad dream but still being affected by it," she says. "I want to believe it was a nightmare and it's over, but I can't yet."

That nightmare is over. Chris's death ensures that it truly is, but it almost certainly means another one is about to begin.

I've just driven back from Atlanta and I'm exhausted. I feel myself shake awake when she starts talking again.

"No more stalking," she says. "No more threats. No more wondering if he's about to break in again and . . ."

Images of Chris holding a gun to Johanna's sweet little head fill my mind. As do ones of me killing him with my own bare, blood-spattered hands.

"Taylor has a chance at a normal life now."

"We're gonna make sure she has an exceptional one," I say.

At that Anna begins to cry.

It starts as a soft, intermittent line of tears streaming down her face but quickly turns into sobs.

I slide over and pull her into me, wrapping my arms around her and holding her tightly as her body convulses.

We stay like this for a while.

I feel as if I'm absorbing all the emotions being released from her being—all the sadness and fear and dread and embarrassment and anger and rage and frustration and disappointment and betrayal and relief and happiness. Everything she has been carrying around for so long is finally flowing out of her. Like a river flooding its banks, she can no longer contain the torrent of feeling that has been rising, building, expanding for these many months.

"I'm sorry," she says between sniffles and sobs. "I know you have to go."

I shake my head. "I don't have to go anywhere."

She stops crying as suddenly as she started and pulls back enough to look at me. "But you've got to get up to the crime scene."

I shake my head. "I can't work this case—even if I wanted to."

"You have to," she says.

"Not only do I have zero desire to work it, it'd be a conflict of interest. I could never—a defense attorney would shred a case where an investigator worked the murder of his wife's ex."

"But—"

"Think about all that Chris has done to us," I say. "All the threats and harassment and attempts at murder."

"Yeah?"

"Chances are someone close to us, who cares about us, killed Chris *for us*," I say.

"That's exactly why you have to work the case," she says.

The little town of Wewahitchka is eerily empty, its streets appearing abandoned in the thick fog.

Nothing is stirring, not a soul in sight, only darkness and a few fog-muted smudges of illumination, the red flashing of the stoplight at the intersection of 22 and 71 seeming to warn of far more than oncoming traffic.

Before leaving home, I had pulled out my phone to call Dad or Merrill to ask one of them to come guard Anna and the girls, but realized with Chris dead there was no need.

Chris is dead.

The reality of it—if it is indeed real—has yet to fully register, but the potential implications have. If it's true it solves certain problems for us—but only as it creates new ones.

I take a left onto Highway 71 and head out of the deserted downtown. My destination is the Dead Lakes Recreational Area about a mile north of Wewa at the end of Gary Rowell Road.

The recreational area, once a state park, is more a campground than anything else, with sites for both tents and RVs. The primary park is on the left side of Gary Rowell, which in addition to camp sites, has nature trails, a playground, picnic pavilions—all around a two acre pond with a fountain at its center and two docks, one covered, extending out into it.

On the right side of Gary Rowell are a smaller pond and a boat launch into the Dead Lakes.

The park is far enough out of town to be its own little world, but close enough that it's convenient for locals to use— though I'm not sure how many actually do on a regular basis. Every Halloween the high school puts on a fundraiser at the park called Haunted Trails, and it seems as though the entire town turns out for what is essentially a very long haunted house in the woods along the park's nature trails. Anna and I attended it last year and absolutely loved it—not just the haunted trail itself but seeing friends and neighbors, hanging out around campfires, taking the girls on a hayride. We also regularly bring Taylor and Johanna to play on the playground and for family cookouts and picnics.

Recently the park had garnered national attention among a certain narrow, niche segment of the population when an elderly man swore he saw Bigfoot on one of the trails near the campground. The story was published on the Backpackerverse website with the headline: A Kind Old Man Swears Bigfoot Lurks At This Florida Campground. In it, the seventy-five year old Michigan man, who is an avid birdwatcher, describes gazing into the woods and seeing something huge pass between two willow trees—something huge that moved fast, was covered in dense, brown hair, and smelled like a wet, dirty dog and rotten meat.

I have been visiting the park since childhood and though I've never seen Bigfoot, I have had some exciting adventures, some great times, and some meaningful experiences at it. I hope what has happened to Chris won't change that.

My phone rings, the vibration in my left pocket in the quiet car on the dark night at nearly four in the morning startling.

I glance down long enough to see it's Merrill, then answer.

"Ding dong, the bitch is dead," he says.

I laugh. "That's what I hear," I say, wondering how he already knows. "Wouldn't have taken you for a *Wizard of Oz* fan."

"That's what that's from? Never knew. Just hear shit and repeat it."

"And put your own spin on it," I add.

"Anybody in this world ever been a bitch, it was him. Gonna break in your house and put a gun to your little girl's head— and that after months of harassing y'all, and *that* after trying to kill your ass. He a bitch."

"You won't get any argument from me," I say.

I cross over West Arm Bridge and can see enough from the spill of my headlights and the street lamps to tell the lakes and therefore the rivers are very high right now.

The beautifully haunting Dead Lakes is a nearly seven-thousand-acre flooded hardwood forest that occurred when the Appalachicola River drifted over and blocked the Chipola River downstream, submerging a huge swath of the cypress swamp and killing the trees, which now rise out of the black, tannic water like the jagged bones of an ancient graveyard.

Merrill says, "I'm hoping you and ol' Sheriff Reg got sense enough to know whoever put the bitch out of our misery did the world a favor and deserves to be left the hell alone."

"You tryin' to tell me somethin'?" I ask.

"Just did."

"Just wanted to make sure I wasn't missing any crucial subtext I was meant to get."

"Never known you to," he says. "The question alone shows your perceptive ass ain't missed anything this time neither."

As soon as I end the call with Merrill, I call the Gulf County jail administrator and ask him to get confirmation that Randa Raffield is still in custody—and was last night when Chris was killed.

"What're you doing here?" Reggie asks.

"I'm not," I say.

"Good. 'Cause you can't be."

She has walked over to where I'm standing in the dark, some fifty feet or so from the circle of light around the crime scene.

It's a hot, dark July night. The air is thick and humid, still and stale, nothing stirring beneath the starless sky. Beyond the bowl of the small lake, the campers and tents on the other side are illuminated by the faint white light of a security lamp and the random dots of nightlights left on both inside and outside the campers. Near one of the tents the embers of a campfire continue to glow.

"Actually, I'm glad you're here," she says. "We're gonna need your help with this one. You'll just have to be unofficial and way, way in the background."

"You saying it's not straightforward or obvious who did it," I say.

Most homicides are. Usually there's no big mystery on how a person was murdered, why, and by whom, but occasionally you catch a baffling murder that presents far more questions than can be answered by even the most thorough of investigations. I've worked both types over the years, but have specialized in the latter.

She nods. "I'm saying without your help, this one's likely to go unsolved."

"Would that be a bad thing?"

"Not necessarily, no, but . . . suspicion is going to fall on you and your family first and our department soon after. I've already heard talk. Now . . . don't get me wrong, it's sympathetic. People are on your side. Everybody understands why you can't let a guy break into your home and put a gun to your little girl's head, but do you want your family to live under that kind of cloud for the rest of your life? I think a big part of what we've got to do is prove you and Anna and your friends and family didn't do it, as well as figure out who did."

"And what if one of us did?" I ask.

She turns and looks at me, and though I can barely see her in the darkness, I can feel the intensity of her penetrative gaze.

After a long moment, she finally shakes her head. "I . . . I'm not . . . I don't know then. I really don't. But I'd think it's better if we find out. Either way—no matter who did it—it's better if we find out than some other agency. 'Cause if we don't or it looks like we're not giving this case our best effort, then FDLE will step in and they'll be the ones not only conducting the investigation but slappin' the cuffs on who they think did it. And that could very well be you or Anna."

I think about what she has said, but only for a moment.

In an instant I am thinking of Anna, hearing her say earlier in the evening before the phone call came that Chris wasn't going to be a problem for us any longer, hearing her say, after the phone call came, that I needed to get *up* instead of *over* to the crime scene, as if she knew where the crime scene was. If she had assumed Chris was killed at his house, as I first did, she would have used the word *over*, but she had instead used *up*—the word I would expect her to use about the Dead Lakes Campground, where his body was actually found and where the crime scene actually is. Did she know? If so, how? I can think of only two ways.

"Regardless of who did it," she says, "regardless of how much it needed to be done . . . aren't we—your family and friends and our department—better off if we conduct the investigation?"

I continue to think about all the implications of the case and my involvement.

"I owe you, John," she says. "Big time. And I'll do whatever you want me to, but I'm reconciled to the fact that I'm going to be a one-term sheriff, so I don't have to calculate the politics or perceptions of my decisions, which is very freeing. Everything I'm saying, I'm saying because I want to do what's best for you, for all of us. I'm calculating the people, not the politics, but like I said . . . I owe you. I'll do whatever you want, but if at all possible I'd like to avoid looking inept or foolish or corrupt."

4

"Take me through it," I say.

Reggie smiles and nods, knowing my request means I plan to work the case from the shadows like she wants me to.

We are waiting for the FDLE crime scene unit to arrive—the only job until then securing the area, protecting evidence.

"Dispatch gets an anonymous call," she says, "but as we're responding to it, Chris's dad calls from Tallahassee, says Chris called him and his mom repeatedly saying he was dying and needed their help."

"I thought Chris's mom was dead and he didn't speak to his dad," I say.

"His dad said he only calls them when he's high or desperate, but this time he sounded sober and genuinely hurt and scared. His folks don't live together. Divorced decades ago. Think he called both of them over and over. Chris's mom is in a nursing home and kept calling his dad until he finally called us."

"Did he tell them anything else, anything about what was happening or who was—"

"Don't think so, but we need to talk to the dispatcher and interview them as soon as we can."

I nod.

"The anonymous caller said a guy is sitting at a picnic table beneath a pavilion at the old state park with a hood tied around his head and a knife sticking out of his heart."

I look over toward the pavilion to see what she's describing.

The pavilion is a pole barn kit constructed on a cement slab —green tin roof on a black metal frame held up by eight enormous posts. Three large wooden picnic tables sit beneath it.

Chris appears to be seated at the center picnic table, his head propped in his right hand, the elbow of which is leaning on the table. His back is to us so I can't see the knife, but even from this distance I can make out dirt and mud and blood on his clothes and on the hood around his head.

The hood, which is cinched around his neck with a narrow piece of white cotton cord, looks like the homemade execution hood of someone about to be hanged.

"Have you confirmed it's Chris and that he's dead?" I ask.

She nods. "I had Jessica video herself lifting the hood just enough to do both then return it to its original position as best she could."

Jessica Young is our crime scene tech. She's here taking pictures and preserving evidence and will assist and liaison with the FDLE crime scene unit and eventually their lab.

The Florida Department of Law Enforcement is a state agency with investigators, crime scene units, forensic labs, and other resources to assist smaller departments in rural counties like ours.

Ours is the very kind of department and this is the very kind of investigation FDLE was designed to assist.

"And he's got a knife still stuck in his heart?" I say.

"A Swiss Army knife, yes," she says. "And he's taken one hell of a beating."

I think about that. "Beaten and stabbed," I say. "Was he shot and hanged too?"

Over near where Jessica is taking pictures of the body in situ, the yawning deputy in charge of the crime scene log is holding a pen and the binder containing the log. His sole responsibility is to keep a written record of everyone who enters the crime scene. I am reasonably certain I have stayed far enough away not to be entered into his log—and I will have to keep it that way.

"Caller wouldn't give his name and wouldn't answer any questions," she continues. "Says he didn't get too close and didn't touch anything, but it was obvious the man was dead."

I look over at the crime scene again.

It is odd and jarring to see Chris just sitting there like he's napping—especially now that the deputies and investigators have stepped away and it's just him, a lone figure, lit as if on a movie set by a bank of portable LED lights the deputies set up, the dark, empty park expanding away behind him.

"Dispatch sent EMS and a deputy out," she is saying. "Deputy was Cody Faircloth."

Cody Faircloth is a young deputy Reggie has received numerous complaints about. So far she's found no evidence of anything criminal or that even rises to the level of a written reprimand, but in addition to being sexist and racist, he's cocky and lazy and does sloppy police work.

"He actually did what he was supposed to do. Secured the area, kept EMS out of the crime scene because it was obvious the victim was dead, called Darlene—she was the investigator on duty—then he called me. Of course, so did she when she got here and saw what it was."

Darlene Weatherly is a short, solid, muscular young woman who I had worked with in Marianna while up there with Dad investigating the Janet Leigh Lester case. She was a frustrated deputy who, because she was a young woman and a lesbian, got the worst assignments and had no hope of advancement. When an investigator's position came open in our department I recommended her to Reggie. She had only been with us a few months.

"You trace the call yet?" I ask.

She shakes her head. "Not yet. Arnie's working on it."

Arnie Ward is the other sheriff's investigator. There are only three in our small department. Me, Arnie, and now Darlene. He's back at the substation working with the cellphone carrier on tracking the phone that was used to report the crime and notifying the provider to protect and save all the data associated with the phone because a court order for it will be forthcoming.

Across the smallish pond I can see people beginning to look out of their campers, gazing at the swirling blue lights of the deputies' cars and the seated man with the hood on his head beneath the picnic pavilion.

"We've got to keep them away," she says. "Let me show you something."

I follow her over toward the pavilion where the body is. Stopping well short of the area where Chris is sitting, she snaps on her flashlight and trains the beam on tracks along the ground. I study them.

They are drag marks from where the killer dragged Chris's body across the damp earth. Though most clearly visible in the dirt they can also be seen in the grass where pine straw, leaves, twigs, and limbs have been raked away by the heels of Chris's shoes.

"Explains the mud and debris on his clothes," I say.

She nods.

"It starts on a small trail way over there," she says, pointing her light to the woods on the other side of the dirt road.

Beyond the narrow dirt road, white from a dusting of lime rock, is a small field where I had participated in three-legged and croaker sack races as a kid. A thick pine woods with dense undergrowth borders the far side of the field. A lone camper sits in the field close to the woods, the drag marks running beside it. Unlike the other campers on the opposite side of the park, this one is not hooked up—there is no hookup here. It's empty and has clearly been parked here temporarily for storage.

Amazingly enough, the first deputy on the scene spotted the drag marks and blood on the road and was able to protect them. To my astonishment no vehicles have driven over the evidence.

"There's blood on the trail and broken branches," she says. "Divots in the dirt, signs of a struggle. Looks like he was executed over there then dragged over here and propped up at the table."

I think about it. "Why put him on display?" I ask. "Why not leave him hidden where he was killed?"

Obviously, the killer wanted him found far more quickly than if he had left him in the woods, but why? Was he also the one who called to report the crime? Is it an act of mocking Chris, taunting us, or something else entirely?

"Exactly," she says. "Why the hood around his head? Why the knife left in his heart? Why up here instead of his house or somewhere in town? What was he doing up here?"

There's that word again. Did Anna know he was *up* here or was it just an innocent turn of phrase?

"Lots of questions," she adds. "I hope forensics can be of some benefit. Soon as FDLE gets here and we get the scene processed, we'll start canvasing the campers and the homes in the area and search the rest of the park."

I nod. "Need to track down whoever made the call that came in," I say. "Talk to him. Could be the killer. At the very least an important witness. What was he doing up here at three in the morning?"

"I'm glad you were in Atlanta," she says. "It's gonna be bad enough to have your friends and family as suspects, but it'll help to not have you on the list."

"It'll depend on time of death," I say. "And you know how questionable and unreliable that can be."

"Why?"

"I didn't go straight home when I got back in town," I say.

"Shit. Where'd you go?"

"Rode by Chris's place," I say.

"And?"

"Got out and—"

"You know what—don't tell me. I don't want to know. I'll come back to you once we have a better idea of time of death. Between now and then get your story straight. Think long and hard about what you're going to say. And don't just think about its veracity but how it's going to sound. That's even more important. That's something we've all got to consider."

I think about what she's said, but don't respond. I'm somewhat surprised by her comments. She seems more concerned about how things look than how they are.

Now that Jessica is finished with the crime scene photographs, two deputies are hanging tarps on the sides of the pavilion to shield the body from view and to preserve evidence until the FDLE crime scene unit can get here.

"Wonder if it's someone close to us?" she says. "Has to be, right? Someone who has seen all the harassment, knows about the attempted murder, knows he broke into your home and held your family at gunpoint."

I think about Dad being just outside the door of the room Chris had us in, about him hearing Chris's threats and seeing him pointing a gun at his son and granddaughter. It would be extremely difficult for a man like him to witness such things and do nothing about them. Of course the same is true of Merrill, Daniel, Merrick, Anna, Sam, Jake, and even Reggie herself. And there are others. Randa Raffield not only threatened to kill Chris, she had actually broken into his home to make good on her promise just before we arrested her. She'd be the prime suspect if she hadn't been in custody at the time he was killed—and even with that we'd still have to investigate her, still have to attempt to rule her out. We had witnessed firsthand feats she had performed that would make killing a man while appearing to be or actually being in custody a modest achievement by comparison.

Reggie starts to say something else, but stops as the FDLE crime scene techs pull up.

"Guess for now all we can do is follow the evidence and see where it leads," she says instead. "And try to figure out what to do about it once we see where that is."

5

As the first glow of false dawn intensifies and gives way to the breaking day, the burst of bright orange along the eastern rim of the park brings the peaceful perfection of this sacred place into full relief.

The tops of the tall pines framing the small pond, picnic pavilions, playground area, and campsites are rust-burnished and sun-kissed. The dew-damp pine needles both on the ground and on the trees glisten in the early morning radiance like a trillion tiny twinkling party lights.

Not even the emergency vehicles, their lights still flashing, the crime scene tape rippling in the breeze, the white-suited forensic techs, nor the bizarrely hooded dead body can take away from the serenity and splendor of this place that has been holy to me since childhood.

What is now known as the Dead Lakes Recreational Area, and used to be the Dead Lakes State Park, is over eighty acres of longleaf pine, magnolia, and bald cypress trees—with a few white tupelos along the wet banks of the Dead Lakes. The quiet, pristine area is comprised of river sways to the east, swamp forest to the north, and pine flatwoods to the west and south.

When I was a kid, and back when it was still a state park, I came here for Boy Scout events. When I was a teenager and dating a girl from Wewa, I used to come here and walk the hiking trails, and on one particularly memorable weekend, I spent most of a dark night of the soul alone in this natural sanctuary.

I'm currently standing in the small field the body had been dragged through. When I was a kid, it had been an empty field used for many fun scouting activities. As a young adult, the field was no longer a field but a planted slash pine forest. Now it is a field again. In my lifetime I had seen an entire crop of trees be planted, grow to maturity, and be harvested, and seen the field come full circle again.

Across the way, where once had been a forest with my favorite section of trail in it, is now a grass-covered slope with a few scattered pine trees forming part of the bowl that contains the lake.

All around me everything is changing as the relentless ticks of time countdown to the time when I, like the forest or the planted pines in the field, am no longer a part of this ebb and flow of birth and life and death, and it will carry on as if I had never been here at all.

How many people who are no longer alive had stood in this same field or visited this same sacred space? How many native or indigenous people had found this same picturesque plot of land just as breathtaking and spiritual as I do? How many witnessed change during their own brief lifetimes and were both saddened and comforted that it would go on changing without them once they were gone?

My phone vibrates in my pocket and I pull it out to see that Anna is calling.

"Morning," I say.

"Morning."

"I'm gonna miss being alive when I'm gone," I say.

"Actually, you probably won't," she says.

"True."

She's right. Either I won't exist at all and therefore have no consciousness to miss consciousness with or I'll still be here in some way, or I'll be on a different plane entirely and so chances are the only grieving and missing I'll do is in the here and now, which is a complete waste of time.

"How's it going there?" she asks.

"Slowly. FDLE is processing the scene. ME investigator is processing the body. Reggie and Darlene and the others are beginning to break down tasks and assignments. I'm mostly in the background watching."

In addition to everything else, deputies and investigators and even Reggie are beginning the canvas—going from camper to camper, interviewing those present, getting their information, taking their statements, asking if they saw or heard anything suspicious the preceding night.

In this instance we're dealing with a fluid and dynamic situation. The campers can load up their RVs and leave at any time. We have no legal reason to detain them. The best we can hope to do is get their contact information and statements before they do.

"I can't believe the girls and I were right there yesterday," she says. "Sat at that very table."

"You were?" I ask. "I didn't know that."

"Thought I told you," she says. "Must have been when you were meeting with Trace."

I had been in Atlanta attempting to close a case—the murder of Mariah Evers, the daughter of the rapper and TV star Trace "Evidence" Evers. Anna and I had spoken several times throughout the day and she had never mentioned bringing the girls here to play.

"I thought we were completely safe there," she is saying. "Thought apart from Bigfoot it was one of the safest places in the world—especially with Merrill watching us."

"Merrill was with you?"

"I wouldn't've gone alone. How tired are you?"

"Delirious."

"Anything I can do?" she asks.

"Spoon with me while I sleep."

"I stand ready to do just that. Whenever you can."

"Then I hope to see you sooner rather than later," I say.

"In a world that no longer includes Chris," she says. "A much better world now. Hurry home. Love you."

"Oh, speaking of . . . Didn't you tell me Chris's mother was dead and that he didn't speak to his father?"

"Yeah. Why?"

"Dispatch seems to think they're both alive and that he spoke to both of them last night."

"Really?"

"Called them for help."

"I keep finding out new things he lied to me about," she says. "Could've lied about his parents, too. But if he did, he did so over a long period of time and very convincingly. Nothing should surprise me from such a sick sociopath, but . . . stuff still does."

When we end the call, Reggie is walking toward me.

"It's more complicated than it looks," she says. "FDLE and the ME are about to walk us through it. You ready?"

6

"There was nothing quick about this," the ME investigator says.

His name is Hanlon. He is a tall, thin man with too-skinny arms, bony fingers, and the grayish pallor of a corpse—except for his beard stubble, which is so dark it looks blue.

"That's true of his time here at the park as well as his murder," Nina, the lead FDLE crime scene investigator, adds.

She is a thickish, thirty-something woman with silky black hair and a dark complexion, her features hinting at some combination of native, Mexican, and/or Eskimo.

At Reggie's request, Nina and Hanlon are walking us through the crime scene now that it has been processed. Reggie, Darlene, Jessica, and I are gathered around them. Arnie will join us when he returns—as will the FDLE agent when he arrives.

When Reggie had called FDLE, they had asked her the same question they always do—Do you want an agent or just the crime scene unit? Because of our department's conflicts and dealings with Chris, she had requested an agent so no one will be able to say we purposefully botched the investigation or concealed evidence or set up someone to take the fall for something one of us had done.

Of course, they can still say it—and probably will—but with FDLE actively involved investigating the case alongside us, it won't have credibility.

"So," Reggie says, "he was here at the park for an extended period of time and his death wasn't quick, is that right?"

"Well, I'm not saying his actual death wasn't relatively quick," Hanlon says. "I'm saying he was beaten and tortured for an extended period of time, probably in and out of consciousness and in severe pain for hours before he actually died."

"Do we have a time of death?" Darlene asks.

Hanlon shrugs and frowns. "We have a range, but . . . it'll be helpful if we can narrow it down in other ways. My best estimate is between ten o'clock PM and three o'clock AM."

As he speaks, she feverishly jots down notes onto a narrow flip-style notepad she had withdrawn from her pocket.

"How about cause of death?" she says.

"We'll have to wait for the autopsy to tell us that," he says. "The victim was beaten, strangled, and stabbed. We won't know for certain which of these actually killed him until we perform the autopsy."

Darlene glances at Reggie then me. "Somebody wanted to make sure he was good and dead," she says. "And that he suffered."

Reggie nods. "And that he was put on display."

"Y'all want to walk through it?" Nina asks.

We indicate we do.

"Okay, so we need to start in the woods over there," she says, pointing across the narrow dirt road and over the field to the woods beyond.

As she leads us over to the woods, she instructs us to be careful of the drag marks and other evidence, even though it is clearly marked and has already been photographed and processed.

"The nature trails are over there by the tent area," she says, turning and nodding to her left. The tent camping area and the starting point of the nature trail are over a hundred yards away. "What's over here is much smaller, not official, could've been made by animals or kids, but I suspect the victim made it—and not just today."

I think about that and the implications of Chris having been up here before, watching from the woods—possibly as Anna and I and the kids had our family cookouts and playdates.

As we continue walking, I notice Cody Faircloth has joined our group, slipped in quietly toward the back as if he's supposed to be with us.

Cody is an early-twenties, blond-haired, green-eyed, shortish young man who appears to spend an inordinate amount of time at the gym and in the tanning bed.

When Reggie sees him, she turns and says, "You need something, Cody?"

"What's over here?" he says. "We going to see where he was killed?"

"*We* are. *You* are going back over to help secure the scene. Keep campers and reporters out of it. Hurry back over there and help Carl."

He stops walking and eventually turns and starts moving back toward the pavilion, but he doesn't hurry. He never does exactly what he's told.

Nina leads us along the drag marks, past the lone RV, and into the woods.

We walk next to the trail instead of on it, through uneven ground and the thick, prickly understory of a healthy, verdant flatwoods forest.

"See how this trail has been trampled and worn relatively

recently," she says. "And we can tell from the shoe prints it was mostly by the same man, the victim, Chris Taunton. Prints here match the shoes he's wearing. It appears he enters these woods up near the entrance to the park and walks far enough back not to be seen by anyone in the park, coming over here and along the length of the pavilions and playground area."

"Like he's stalking," Darlene says.

"Fits with what we already know about him," Reggie says.

"If that's what he was doing," Nina says, "then at some point the predator became prey. Look at this."

She points to blood on the base of a smallish magnolia tree and the ground in front of it—all of which is marked by bright yellow crime scene markers.

"See the hair and blood on the bark," she says. "I think his head was slammed into the tree with tremendous force."

"That's consistent with some of the wounds on the back of his head," Hanlon says.

"So he's standin' here," Darlene says, "and someone comes up behind him, grabs his head, and slams it into the base of the tree?"

"That's possible," Nina says. "But so is rushing at him and slamming him into it from the front. His body could've hit first and then his head snapped back and smacked it. However it happened, you can see from the marks on the ground that whoever did it pummeled him once he was on the ground."

"So the blow to his head dazes him and he falls to the ground," Darlene says, "out of it or unconscious and the killer jumps on him and starts beating the shit out of him?"

"It's possible. Or his attacker could've just stood here kicking and stomping him."

"Then pulls out a knife and stabs him," Darlene says, "then drags his body over to the pavilion and props him up at the table?"

"No," Nina says. "This is only one of many assaults the

victim underwent. Let's follow the blood trail and I'll show you what I mean."

She leads us along the path, our eyes trained on the drops and smears of blood on the blades of grass, dirt, leaves, and twigs on the trail.

Eventually, we arrive at another area where there are more signs of struggle and more blood.

"So he's badly beaten, concussed, dazed," Darlene says, "and he tries to crawl away along the trail, but he only gets so far before the killer starts assaulting him again. Like he's playing with him, prolonging it, dragging out the pain and suffering and the mental torture of knowing he's about to die."

"It's possible," Nina says.

"There's nothing in the body of evidence to contradict something like that," Hanlon says, "but based on what I've seen I'd say we're talking several hours, perhaps most of the day. It'll take the autopsy to tell us for sure, but it appears to me from some of the bruising and the appearance of some of the wounds that the prolonged attack could've taken up to ten hours or more."

I wonder what time Anna and Merrill and the girls were here.

"So for hours he's crawling along this trail being taunted and tortured by his killer," Darlene says. "That's some pretty sadistic shit."

Reggie says, "You're jumping to far too many conclusions. Let's hear all the evidence—including from the autopsy and other sources before we come up with hard and fast theories."

"Sorry," she says. "My bad. Rookie mistake. Obviously, I'm trying too hard."

"You're doing great," I say. "It's just easy to draw conclusions from partial evidence that aren't supported by the totality of the evidence. We've all done it."

"The problem is," Reggie says, "a lot of times you never see anything else because early theories blind you to what the entirety of the evidence says. All that being said . . . our two forensic experts are saying the evidence so far supports the conclusions you're drawing."

Nina and Hanlon nod and Hanlon says, "Best to wait for the autopsy before drawing any definitive conclusions."

Regardless of what other evidence or the autopsy shows, Darlene is right about one thing—Chris suffered. He hadn't just been murdered. He had been tortured.

"If you'll come over this way," Nina is saying, "we'll show you where we believe he was actually killed."

She leads us along the trail to another spot beneath an immature oak tree with even more blood on it and the ground around it.

"See the blood on the base of the tree?" she says. "We think he was either propped up here by the killer or leaned up against it himself. And it seems like he was here for quite a while. And the reason we believe he was killed or finally died here was because this is the spot his body was dragged from over to where we found him."

"Not trying to jump to conclusions or anything," Darlene says, "but could it be the killer was waiting until it got late enough so no one would see him move the body and leave the park? He just left him here until the coast was clear."

"That's possible," Nina says. "You're probably right, but what I'm also saying is he spent a lot of time here while he was still alive. He bled a good bit onto the base of that tree for an extended period of time."

"And," Hanlon adds, "dead men don't bleed."

"Speaking of bleeding," Hanlon says as we're making our way back out of the woods, "remember how I told you some of the victim's injuries were inflicted long enough before death to actually start healing?"

"Yeah?" Reggie says.

"Others were inflicted far enough after death not to bleed."

We are all moving slowly through the woods, next to but not on the trail of Chris's blood, working our way back toward the place where we entered and ultimately back to the pavilion area.

"We actually have ante, peri, and postmortem wounds, injuries, and trauma present," he adds.

"Sorry," Darlene says, "but am I the only one who needs to pull out my phone and look up the definitions of what he just said?"

"Antemortem means *before* bodily functions ceased," he says. "Perimortem means *at* or *around* the time of death. And postmortem means *after* death."

"Yeah, I knew that last one," Darlene says.

"The body not only underwent a significant amount of trauma," Hanlon says, "but over three distinct time periods."

Reggie says, "I know we've got to wait for the autopsy for exact results, but can you tell us approximately which wounds were inflicted when?"

"Only in the most general terms," he says. "We really do need to wait for the autopsy to be precise, but . . . I'd say the majority of the blunt force trauma—the assault, the beating—was antemortem." He gives a quick glance to Darlene. "Before death."

She nods. "Got it."

"I should add that, based on what I've seen so far, an instrument was used for at least some of the assault," Hanlon says.

"An instrument?" Darlene asks.

"Something other than hands and fists," he says. "Though I think they were used too. Again, we'll know more and be able to say more with certainty—"

"*After the autopsy*," Darlene says.

"Exactly," he says with a smile that wrinkles up the gray skin of his skinny face and causes the blue hue of his stubble to shift around a bit, "but my best guess for now is that hands, fists, and something like a bat or a piece of rounded wood and a hammer or some type of small metal mallet was also used."

"Damn," Darlene says.

"And that was mostly done antemortem?" Reggie says.

"Mostly, maybe even exclusively," he says, "though it was likely perimortem as well. But there doesn't appear to be those type injuries that are postmortem."

"Which are?" Reggie asks.

"All or most of the stab wounds appear to be," he says.

"Someone stabbed a dead man?" Darlene says.

"Someone stabbed a dead man twelve times," he says. "And left the knife in him."

We are all quiet, presumably thinking about that, and I notice our pace slows even more as we do.

"I could've missed some," Hanlon says. "There may be more, but I counted twelve postmortem stab wounds—including the one the knife was left in."

"The killer was smart enough to leave the knife in the body," Reggie says. "Wonder if somewhere in these woods we'll find a bloody bat and a hammer?"

I nod. "Need to start a wider search."

I've tried not to say anything since I'm not supposed to be here and I instantly regret stating the obvious.

"Yes we do," she says.

She starts to say something else, but we hear raised and angry voices coming from the park and pick up our pace again.

As we emerge from the trail, we can see a deputy restraining an elderly man who looks like he could be Chris in thirty years.

8

A s Reggie rushes over to deal with the elderly man who is clearly Chris's dad, I hang back and actually walk in the opposite direction, trying not to be seen.

Stepping behind the RV in the small field next to the trail where Chris had been killed, I drift over to a spot where I can hear and see what's going on without being seen.

"I just want to know if that's my son," Lyle Taunton is saying. "You can damn sure tell me that. I've driven all the way from Tallahassee."

Lyle Taunton's pale, parchment-thin skin is puffy and red-splotched. His sparse, fine white hair is oiled and combed to the side. His body is that of an old man—slightly bent with a big belly hanging over his belt and the overall appearance of stiffness. And though it's July hot, he has a sweater on. The resemblance to his son is striking. It's as if we're looking at an older, thicker, live version of Chris.

"Mr. Taunton," Reggie says, as she walks up, "I'm Reggie Summers. I'm the sheriff."

"*You?*"

"Yes."

"You're the sheriff?"

"Yes, sir, I am."

It seems Lyle is as sexist as his son was.

Beyond where they're standing at the far edge of the crime scene tape, I can see that a couple of local TV news camera crews have arrived and set up.

"I want you to know that I understand where you're coming from and what you want to know," she says. "I'd want to know the same thing if I were in your position. But we don't have a positive ID yet and we can't say for sure until we do. Please try to see it from our perspective. How bad would it be, how painful for a family or loved one if we told them their loved one was deceased when they weren't or that they weren't when they really were."

"Well, sure, but—"

"That said, I will tell you this," she says. "While we don't have a positive ID, we do believe the victim is Chris Taunton."

The old man's knees buckle and he collapses, the deputy reaching for him and easing his fall.

No matter how much of a monster a person becomes they're still someone's child. Someone will be shocked or saddened or affected in some way by their death.

I think about the fact that we haven't found any ID on Chris and wonder where his wallet and phone and keys are.

All through the morning my phone has been vibrating—alerting me to calls, texts, and voicemails—but so far I've not been able to even look at it. But now, as Reggie and the others are tending to Lyle Taunton and I'm trying to stay out of sight of the cameras, I pull my phone out and scroll through the various notifications.

I have missed several calls and numerous texts from Anna, Dad, Merrill, Jake, Daniel, Sam, Merrick, and Susan.

Though I try to push it away the moment it arrives unbidden, I think *There's your primary suspects list right there.*

Some of them have more of a motive than others, and some are more likely to do it than others, but a case can be made for each of them to be suspected.

Anna has perhaps the strongest motive of all. She's not only the wronged wife, the one he attempted to murder, the object of his obsessive stalking and harassing and threatening, but she's the mom who, with her child, was held at gunpoint. I hope she didn't do it, hope she isn't capable of what was done to Chris, but I would certainly understand if she did.

Speaking of moms, Susan also has a motive. It was our little girl's precious head that Chris held the gun to.

Dad was there, right outside the door when Chris was holding us hostage in Taylor and Johanna's room. He heard everything, witnessed firsthand the threat this sick, narcissistic, deranged man was to our family. He's also the one who intervened and disarmed Chris when he finally brought us out of that room. He had knocked the gun out of Chris's hand and subdued him, but had certainly looked like he wanted to do more.

Merrill, of course, would do it for me, for us, for friendship, to protect us, perhaps even to do it before we did.

To a lesser extent the others might have done it for the same reasons—or for personal motives I know not of.

As I'm trying to decide who, if anyone, to call back, a call comes in and makes the decision for me. It's Dad. I take it.

"Hey," I say.

"You still at the scene?"

"Yeah. Sort of. I'm in the background."

"Don't stay too far in the background," he says. "Be a good idea for you to be involved in this one."

"Anna said the same thing,"

"She's right. Listen to her. That slimy son of a bitch being dead is a good thing. Don't let it turn into a bad thing for the person with big enough balls to do what needed to be done."

I think about what he's saying, and though there's a lot in it, my primary focus is on the implication that if I didn't kill Chris it was because I didn't have the balls, or big enough balls, to do what needed to be done.

Should I have been the one to extinguish Chris's flame? Did I let someone else do what I should have done? Was it my responsibility since he was threatening my family? Were my efforts to keep them safe without doing anything illegal or immoral too little, too safe, too lacking in balls—is that what he's implying?

What kind of man lets another man try to kill him and his wife, lets him harass and stalk and threaten, lets him break into his home and hold a gun on his family and doesn't put that man down?

What kind of man lets someone else do that for him?

"I've got to go, Dad," I say.

"Remember what I said. Protect whoever did it. It's the least you can do for them."

9

Arnie Ward arrives with the phone information just ahead of Tony Ford, the FDLE agent assigned to assist us in the investigation.

Reggie turns Lyle Taunton over to Darlene, and she, Arnie, and Tony drift over toward me in the field.

Hidden by the empty RV, she makes the introductions, explains the situation and my presence to Tony, who tells us he goes by Ford, then asks Arnie what he found out about the phone.

"The call was made from right here in the park," he says. "Phone belongs to a Howard Thompson."

"We need to talk to the campground host and see if Howard Thompson is staying here," Reggie says.

She takes off immediately toward the campground area of the park, the three of us falling in line behind her and following.

The host manages the campground for the county and lives in an RV centrally located next to the cinderblock bathhouse.

Reggie steps up on the black metal steps and knocks on the camper door.

In a moment, the door is opened by a thin, middle-aged hippie with a long gray ponytail, a female version of himself hovering over his left shoulder.

Reggie introduces herself and asks if he's the camp host.

"Sure am," he says. "I'm HC and this is my wife Georgia."

"Can't believe you found a body in our park," Georgia says. "Do you know who it is yet? Is she one of our guests?"

Reggie shakes her head. "We don't think the victim was staying in the park."

"Well, that's a relief."

"And the victim is male."

"Oh."

"But we *are* looking for someone who might be staying here," she says. "A Howard Thompson."

They both start laughing.

"What's so funny?" Reggie asks.

"I'm Howard Thompson," he says. "Howard Carter Thompson. I go by HC. How can I help?"

"Did you call 9-1-1 to report the body over under the pavilion?"

He shakes his head. "Didn't know about it until one of our guests knocked on my door this morning and told me and I stepped out and seen all the flashing lights over there."

"You sure you didn't call?"

"Positive. I'd know if I did. My brain's not that fried. Not yet."

"Could someone have used your phone to do it?" Reggie asks.

He glances over his shoulder at his wife.

She shakes her head. "Don't look at me. Got my own damn phone."

He looks back at us and shrugs. "Guess not."

"Do you have your phone on you?" Arnie asks. "May I take a look at it?"

"Absolutely, officer. It's not a problem."

As HC extracts the phone from the front left pocket of his multicolored flared carpet pants, Arnie quickly snaps on a pair of latex gloves.

"I'm assuming you want me to unlock it," HC says as he thumbs in his passcode.

"Yes, sir, thank you," Arnie says.

As Arnie studies the phone, I glance back around behind me at the park. The hot July sun looms in the midmorning sky, beating down on us, causing our exposed skin to sting and perspire.

"What carrier is this phone with?" Arnie asks.

"Verizon," HC says.

"The phone we're looking for is with AT&T," he says. "Do you have a second phone—one with them?"

He nods slowly. "Had an AT&T phone when we first got here," he says. "Signal for it around here was for shit so got a new one with Verizon."

"Where is that other phone?" Reggie asks. "Do you still have it?"

He squints and his small eyes nearly disappear. "What did I do with that other phone?" he says, looking up, seeming to access memories.

"Bet it's in the other camper," Georgia says.

"You know . . . I think you're right," he says.

"What other camper?" Reggie asks.

"The one parked over there," he says, leaning out of the doorway a little more and pointing toward the RV in the field next to where Chris was murdered. "We been hosting a long time—move from park to park. Picked up a couple of campers along the way. That one's ours too. It's not hooked up right now. Just sort of sitting over there for now. We keep some things in it —storage kind of stuff."

When HC, who is wearing latex gloves now, starts to unlock the door to his RV near the crime scene, we can tell the door is not only unlocked but ever so slightly ajar.

"I should have noticed that before," I say.

"We all should have," Reggie says. "But we were looking down at the bloody drag marks."

HC starts to ease open the door, but Arnie stops him.

"Let us go in first," he says. "Once we know it's clear, we'll let you come in and tell us if anything is missing."

HC steps away from the door to a safe distance out of the line of sight of the door. Arnie, Tony, Reggie, and I all pull our weapons, spread out, and prepare to enter the RV.

Standing to the side, Arnie opens the door and says, "Gulf County Sheriff's Department. Anyone inside?"

There's no response.

"Is there anyone in here?" he says. "This is the Gulf County Sheriff's Department. We are armed. Come out with your hands up. Now."

No response. No movement. Nothing to indicate there's anyone inside.

He and Ford both enter the RV, each facing a different direction, guns drawn, sweeping, clearing, checking.

As they move deeper inside, Reggie and I step in and do essentially the same thing, careful not to point our weapons at Arnie and Ford.

It only takes a few moments for us to know the small RV is empty.

"Clear," Arnie says.

"All clear," Ford says.

As we look around we can see the place, though not ransacked, has been searched—several drawers are open, a cardboard box with electrical cords spilling out of it is turned over on the counter, pieces of rope like the one tied around the victim's neck are in a pile next to kitchen shears on the little dining table, and various other items are strewn about, mostly on the floor.

"Looks like we've got yet another crime scene for FDLE to process," Reggie says.

Arnie steps to the narrow door. "Mr. HC," he says, "would you step in here and just stand right here in the entrance, and without touching, anything look around real quick?"

HC steps in and does just that.

"Somebody's been in here," HC says. "It was nothing like this. All messy, shit scattered about. It was tidy and orderly."

"Where would the phone have been?" Ford asks.

HC nods toward the cardboard box turned over on the countertop. "In there."

"Can you tell if anything else is missing or out of place?" Arnie says.

HC looks around. "That pillow over there had a pillowcase on it. Now it's gone."

"What color was it?" Arnie asks.

"Just a plain white pillowcase," HC says. "Nothing special about it."

"Our hood," Reggie whispers to me.

I nod. "Means the killer didn't come prepared," I say. "May not have even come to kill him, so had to improvise with what he could find in here."

"Mr. HC, do you recall if you might have had a bat or piece of wood or a hammer in here?" Arnie asks.

"Is that what was used to kill him?" he asks. "I know, I know, you can't tell me. Anyway, not that I remember. Maybe a little hammer, but not a bat. Least not that I recall."

10

As FDLE processes HC's extra RV and investigators and deputies canvas the park and surrounding area and I'm trying to remain inconspicuously in the background, a face from the past pops up over near the crime scene tape at the entrance to the park.

I feel ashamed the moment I see her, and as I walk over toward her I think about all the ways I've let her down and ask myself not for the first time how I had allowed it to happen.

Carla Jean Pearson had always just been Carla to me—in the same way her dad had always just been Rudy.

It had been a while since I had seen her. In that time, she had become a young woman. She is still smallish with blond hair and big green eyes, but she is thicker now, more filled out, and if possible, even more world-weary.

I duck beneath the crime scene tape and wrap her up in a big hug, instantly feeling the difference in her body. And it's not just that she's no longer the teenager who has always been like a daughter to me. Something else is going on with her. I can see it in the fullness and bloom of her figure and the glow of her countenance. I hope I'm wrong but fear I'm not.

"Hey stranger," she says.

"Hey," I say. "It's so good to see you. What're you doing here?"

"What's going on?" she asks, nodding toward the crime scene.

I glance at the reporters and gawkers along the tape and motion for her to follow me away from the small crowd.

"We found a body in one of the pavilions last night," I say.

"Who?"

"Chris Taunton," I say.

"*Anna's ex, Chris Taunton?*" she says.

I nod. "He was murdered."

"Oh my God," she says. "That's . . . so . . . I'm not sure what that is exactly. Not really surprising. Doesn't really make me sad. But . . . I don't know. It's a shock, I guess."

I nod. "It certainly is. What're you doing here?"

"Looking for you," she says.

It may be the first time she has ever lied to me.

"You never come see me anymore," she adds. "I have to come track you down at a crime scene."

Her voice is playful, but her words hold real sadness.

I used to spend almost all night every night with Carla— before I abandoned her for Anna and a happier life.

Carla worked the overnight shift at Rudy's, her dad's 24-hour diner in Pottersville, where I used to live. Since I didn't sleep much and was single, I'd sit in the back booth and read, keeping an eye on the place while she slept between customers.

Carla had been a deeply sad but equally strong motherless young woman being raised by an absentee alcoholic father. In many ways I was all she had, and despite my best intentions and inconsistent efforts, I had become just as absent as her father.

It had started when Anna and I had finally gotten together. It had been completed when we moved from Pottersville to

Wewa. I told myself I would visit, that I would keep a close eye on her, that I wouldn't abandon her like everyone else had, but I had done just that.

I should have insisted she move with us, that we adopt her or become her legal guardians or something, but instead I had gotten busy with a new job and new family and having a full and fulfilling life, and though I hadn't forgotten about her, I had in every way that matters abandoned her.

Standing here with her now I am so overcome with guilt I'm finding it hard to think of anything else.

"How are you?" I ask.

She has always had the saddest eyes. Big, beautiful Gulf-green eyes, but deep and distant and sad too. Now, probably because of my actions—or rather inaction—where she's concerned, they're even more distant, far more sad.

"I'm fine," she says. "You didn't kill Chris, did you?"

Before I can respond she rushes on.

"I mean, I wouldn't blame you if you did. No one would, but . . . I just wouldn't want you to ruin your life for . . . over somebody like him. Of course, you're the law around here, right? So even if you did, you could . . . I'm gonna stop talking now."

"Carla," I say. "I'm so sorry I haven't kept in better touch with you. I meant to. I really did."

Raising herself in the small town poverty of the rural route Deep South, what chance did Carla have? What chance for happiness, for fulfillment, for a life other than the tiny impoverished one she's always known? I had always thought her strength and her good sense and keen mind, along with just a little help here and there, would be her chance.

And I had failed to do my part. Failed at giving her that chance—the chance of parole from the invisible prison she had been born into.

"You live in a different town now," she says. "Have a wife and a new job and daughters of your own."

Daughters of your own. Those four words say it all. She had felt like a daughter of mine and I had treated her like that until I got *daughters of my own.*

My eyes start stinging and I blink back tears.

"No," I say. "There is no excuse. I'm wrong and I'm sorry. Please forgive me. Please give me the chance to make it up to you, to be in your life again. All of us. I'd love for Johanna and Taylor to have a cool, kind, goodhearted big sister to look up to."

Now she is the one blinking back tears.

"I could use a family right now," she says. "I really could. I'm sure it'd do me more good than them, but . . . I'd love to be in their lives."

"I miss our late nights at Rudy's," I say.

"Me too," she says, a stray tear streaking down her pale, smooth cheek.

"I'm not sure how long I'm gonna be here," I say. "Can you hang around and let me take you to lunch?"

She shakes her head. "I wish I could. I would love that more than anything, but . . . I've got a doctor's appointment this afternoon."

"Are you okay?" I ask.

"I'm fine," she says, then turning to the side and pulling the loose fabric of her shirt back, "I'm just pregnant."

"*Pregnant?* Oh wow."

It's one of the things I had always feared for her—getting pregnant, dropping out of school, getting caught in a trap of her own making that she could never quite get free of again.

"Congratulations," I say. "That's wonderful."

The truth is I can't imagine it's wonderful for her—not given her circumstances, her age, her options, her history of bad boyfriends—but I know it can become something wonderful, something life-altering and love-restoring, and I hope it will be.

"You have to let us take you out to celebrate," I say. "Are you free for dinner?"

She nods slowly. "I can be. Absolutely."

"I'll call you this afternoon to—"

"I have a new number," she says.

Has it been that long since I called her? Do I not even have her number anymore? A new wave of guilt washes over me.

I pull out my phone. "Give it to me and I'll program it in," I say.

But as she begins reciting it to me, my phone vibrates. It's Reggie.

"It's the sheriff," I say. "Let me—"

"Go ahead. Take it."

I do.

"Where are you?" Reggie asks.

"Over near the entrance to the park," I say.

"We found a blood-covered bat," she says.

"Oh shit," someone behind her says. "Is that a—"

"And apparently another body," she says.

11

I hurry back over, through the field, past the RV being processed by the crime scene unit from FDLE, and along the trail of blood left by Chris.

Deputies continue to search the woods on either side of the path, slowly poking around the undergrowth with metal rods and rakes.

A few of them point in the general direction of where Reggie is, though she is not visible yet.

A faint walking path of slightly pushed down grass branches off the trail Chris had been on and runs much farther back into the swamp.

As I continue, the terrain becomes far more dense and difficult to traverse, and my pace slows greatly.

As the ground slants down toward the river swamp it grows increasingly damp, muddy, and mucky. The air is far more moist here, filled with far more mosquitos.

The first spot I arrive at is where the bat has been found.

The area around the bat has been taped off and a large yellow evidence marker is teepeed next to it on the ground.

A single deputy stands next to the scene to both make and preserve it.

Given its distance from where Chris had been killed I'd say the killer slung it back here, sending it sailing over the short trees to come to rest back here in the dark, dank dirt.

I squat down a few feet away and study the bat.

It's an old, almost antique wooden Louisville Slugger, more narrow than modern bats, and it's splattered with blood.

To my horror there is something familiar about the bat.

I think I may have seen it before, but I'm not sure where. I'll have to give it a good think later when I have the time—though it's not something I relish doing.

Leaving behind the bat and the alarms it was setting off in my mind, I continue deeper into the sweltering swamp.

I've only taken a few steps when it hits me, the unmistakable stench of death, that smell that signifies sadness and loss and the cruel, indignant, fetid fragrance of decay.

Given that I haven't eaten and haven't slept and I'm in a swamp in July in Florida, I have to stop a moment to swallow against my gag reflex and the bile roiling around inside me, threatening to erupt at any moment.

I hold my nose and breathe through my mouth—slow, deep, cleansing breaths that can't cleanse the smell or its source, but for the moment keep me from throwing up.

I start moving again on unsteady legs, pushing my way through the thick, unwelcoming underbrush of the unforgiving swamp.

When I finally arrive at the scene, I find Reggie, a deputy, and Hanlon.

The deputy is stretching crime scene tape around the surrounding trees. Reggie is standing well away, observing, waiting for me. Hanlon is kneeling near the body.

Reggie turns to me as I approach.

"You okay?" she asks.

I nod.

"You look—"

"Exhausted, hungry, and dehydrated?" I offer.

"Or something like it."

I'm staring at her, my eyes locked in on hers, avoiding the decomposing body mere feet away. When she looks back down toward the body, I take a moment, then slowly will my eyes toward where they don't want to go.

What I see first is a matted nest of long, thick black hair. It's piled in dirt and leaves and upon initial glance doesn't appear to be attached to a head, to a body.

But it is.

The pile of hair is attached to the head of a young woman whose dead body has been partially disinterred from its shallow grave.

"She's been here a while," Hanlon says. "Few weeks at least."

"So she has nothing to do with Chris," Reggie says.

"All we can say for sure is whatever happened to her didn't happen today," I say. "Chris could've buried her out here previously. Or whoever killed Chris could be using this area for a dumping ground. Though given how different they are, they're likely not connected at all."

She nods.

"She was in a relatively shallow grave," Hanlon is saying. "Buried before the water came up, then as it receded some I'd say it shifted the ground and left her partially exposed. Animals have begun to unearth her, but haven't gotten very far yet. We found her just in time."

I know what he means. He's speaking from a forensics standpoint, but I still can't help but think we got to her far too late to help her, to save her, to make any kind of meaningful difference to her.

"We'll get the team in here, process the scene, get her out of the ground," he says. "Won't be able to tell much more until then."

"Thank you," Reggie says to him, then looks around.

I follow her gaze.

We're standing in the midst of a cypress swamp, surrounded by the swollen bases of the craggy trees and a graveyard of cypress knees nearby.

"He brought her a good ways back in here," she says.

I nod. "Unlike whoever killed Chris, he didn't want her found."

"Doesn't mean it can't be the same person," she says. "Different victims. Different MOs."

"Possibly," I say. "It's also possible Chris killed her. But it's probable that it has nothing to do with Chris or his death."

She nods. "I want you to work it," she says. "And not just because everyone else is already working Chris's case, but because it will give you a legitimate reason to remain involved in that investigation. Officially, you're working this case, not the other case, but they already intersect just by virtue of finding them in the same location. And it's possible they'll intersect even more in the near future . . . so . . . you've got to stay in the loop on Chris's."

I nod again. "You're the boss."

"And though you're only officially working one of the investigations," she says. "I'm gonna need you to solve both."

I smile.

"I'm not kidding. We need to know the whats and hows and whos of both cases—especially Chris's. What we do about it after that is another matter entirely."

12

"They found the phone in the camper," Arnie says. "FDLE crime tech. It was only used to make that one call. Killer must have seen it when he broke in to get the bat and rope and stuff, used it after he had set the victim up at the table, then tossed it back in the camper. Before that, it had been almost a week since the phone had been used to place or receive a call."

It's later in the day. I'm so tired I'm lightheaded.

Reggie has gathered all the investigators together for a discussion of what we have and what we know so far. Arnie, Darlene, myself, Reggie from our department. Ford and Nina from FDLE and Hanlon from the ME's office.

Darlene says, "So the killer comes completely unprepared. Has to break into the RV to get shit to use to do the deed."

We are in a sort of circle under a stand of tall pines near the tent area. The narrow, sparse trees are no match for the early afternoon sun, and I can feel sweat snaking down my neck and back.

"That's possible," Tony Ford said, "but it's also possible the killer brought some things and found others. HC says there was no bat in the RV."

"Y'all keep saying *brought*," Reggie says. "But maybe the killer didn't bring anything because he was already here. Could be one of the campers."

"True," Darlene says.

"We're getting statements and contact info from everyone here," Ford says. "We've asked them to let us know before they leave."

"Once we have all the statements typed up and in the murder book I want everyone to read them," Reggie says. "Study them carefully. Look for inconsistencies or anything suspicious. See who we need to talk to again. There's every chance the killer is one of them."

I feel as though my thinking is running at half speed, like there's a lag between what I'm hearing and how I process it and what I think about it.

"There's a lot of staging involved in Chris's murder," I say.

Everyone looks at me.

"We've got to find out why. Why the body was moved. Why the postmortem wounds. Why the hood. Why the displaying of the body."

I feel like what I've said is disjointed and doesn't fit with the flow of the conversation that preceded it, like a person incapable of reading social cues that just blurts out random non sequiturs.

Hanlon says, "I don't remember seeing this much postmortem activity on a victim before."

"Means it's got to be significant, right?" Darlene says.

I nod.

"Think about how different it is from the disposal of the female victim we found in the swamp," Nina says. "One is hidden, only accidentally discovered, the other boldly displayed and accompanied by a phone call that draws attention to it. One is brutal in the extreme, the other—"

"Do we know cause of death on the—do we have a name

for her yet?" Reggie asks. "Any ID?"

Hanlon shakes his head. "No ID. I can tell you she's a young Caucasian woman between the ages of . . . I'd say sixteen and twenty or so . . . with long, thick, coal-black hair and big, round, blue-blue eyes. It's just a guess but I'd say she's been both dead and in the ground for between eight and twelve weeks, but that's just a guess—like most of this. She doesn't appear to have any wounds beside the one that killed her, doesn't appear to have been raped or assaulted. We'll have to wait for the autopsy to be sure, but it appears she died from a single gunshot wound to the head."

"So one is cold and calculating, quick and efficient," Darlene says, "the other passionate, prolonged, torturous."

"We thinking two different killers? Reggie asks. "Are these two homicides unrelated?"

"Nothing to say the same killer didn't do both," I say, "but it certainly seems unlikely. If the same killer didn't kill them both we have to determine whether they're related or connected in any way."

"Hard to imagine two murders so close together not being," Arnie says, "but . . ."

"Okay," Reggie says. "That means we've got to keep an open mind about everything. Follow the evidence. Wait for the autopsy results. And most of all communicate with each other. Darlene and Tony will be working Chris's murder and John and Arnie will have the female victim, but share everything with each other because they might be connected. Probably are. I'm not gonna micromanage you, but this is going to get a lot of attention and scrutiny, so keep me in the loop, run things past me. Let me help you however I can."

We all nod our understanding and assent.

"Now, go get some food and drink and sleep if you need it," she says. "Don't forget a murder investigation is a marathon, not a sprint. John, you look terrible. Go home to Anna."

13

Anna

On the day Chris was killed, Anna awoke with a deep, disturbing sense of dread, trying to remember if she had been having a bad dream, hoping a nightmare was the cause of her feelings of foreboding.

Though more practical and less spiritual than John, she nonetheless trusted her feelings, her impressions, her intuitions—particularly when it came to her children, her family.

Something wasn't right. She knew it—no matter how hard she tried to convince herself otherwise.

She went through her morning rituals, caring for her girls and her home, hoping John would be back from Atlanta sooner than she knew he would, all the while a heaviness, a darkness, just beneath and behind everything.

The dread made her fearful for John's trip to Atlanta—both the travel and his activities there—but as she thought about and prayed for him, she became convinced what she was fretting over had nothing to do with his trip.

It was Chris. It had to be. But what was he going to do this time? What more could he do?

That last question bothered her the most. If he continued to escalate, the more he could do was actually further harm or even kill one of them.

Thinking of the harm he had inflicted led her inevitably to thoughts of Taylor—and what she knew that no one else did. Not even John.

And those thoughts led inevitably to wanting Chris Taunton dead. What mother wouldn't want the monster who harmed her child dead—even or especially when that monster is her child's own father?

She tried hard to push those thoughts away, but it was hard when she and her daughters were actually being protected by armed guards. John's dad, Jack, and John's brother, Jake, were taking rotating shifts with Merrill and Daniel and Merrick in case Chris tried to break in again while John was away, and it infuriated her.

She was angry at the intrusion, at the invasion of privacy, at the loss of freedom, at her need and dependency. She was a strong, capable woman. No one would or could do more to protect her girls than her. She didn't need watching over. But she did. She felt better when they were here—something that made her the most angry of all.

Think about all the good.

We're still here.

But so is he.

She finally had the life she'd always wanted—except for two things, each related to the other.

Don't think about that right now, she tells herself.

Think about all that's good, that's right.

John Jordan is the man of her dreams. She loves and adores

him, respects and admires him, yearns and burns for him. She appreciates who he is—and also because of all the ways in which he is nothing like Chris.

Chris is weak. John is strong. Chris is narcissistic and self-centered. John is genuinely generous and compassionate. She's never met a more empathetic man. Chris is ignorant and arrogant. John is brilliant and humble. Chris is impulsive and immature. John is thoughtful and wise.

But.

As good as John is, as much good as he does every single day, he has certain overarching ideals that often conflict with each other.

John wants to simultaneously save the world and police it. But that's impossible. She loves him for wanting to, for trying so hard to, but she sometimes gets frustrated with him.

His moral code, that sense of justice and honor, of right and wrong that is as much a part of his make up as his DNA is, is at times at odds with the love and compassion and mercy that is perhaps even more fundamental to every single particle that constitutes his being.

Throughout this entire ordeal John has tried to do the right thing as he sees it. She can always count on him for that. But what if the right thing is something he's unable or unwilling to do?

What if the moral thing is the immoral one? What if life is only going to be possible through death? What then? Will the woman who resents having to be watched over have to be the one to do something about it? Will the mother who's responsible both for the safety of her children and for introducing the monster into their lives have to be the one to remove him? If so, so be it. She can do it. She can. Just as naturally and easily and with no more thought or guilt than a mother grizzly protecting her cubs.

14

The drive from the Dead Lakes Recreational Area to our home isn't much over three miles. Driving home I nod off four different times.

When I get home, I hug and kiss Anna, Johanna, and Taylor, talk very briefly with Anna, then go undress and fall into bed.

My dreams are filled with murder.

In each instance I'm working cases I can't solve.

Mariah Evers. Martin Fisher. The young women flung off Stone Mountain by the Stone Cold Killer. Janet Leigh Lester. Shane McMillan.

In every case I have all the information I need, I just can't figure out how it fits together. It's frustrating, infuriating, maddening, but even though I have all the evidence, can see all the various pieces, I am unable to put the puzzle together.

I wake disoriented and dehydrated, head pounding, back sore, agitated, irritable, angry.

Fumbling for my phone in the dark room I realize I forgot to take it out of my pocket and place it on the bedside table.

Leaning down over the side of the bed, I reach into my left front pants pocket and retrieve it, only to discover it's dead.

Stumbling to the door, I yell for Anna.

I can hear my agitation and irritability in my tone.

When she yells back from the other end of the house that she's on her way, I ask her to bring me some water, and amble back over and collapse into bed.

When Anna arrives she finds me trying to plug the small charger cable into my phone. My frustration and lack of patience is obvious.

"Here, I'll do that," she says, taking the phone and handing me the water. "You drink this."

She has left the bedroom door open presumably so she can hear the girls and a swath of light from the hallway provides a little illumination.

Inserting the small connector into the phone quickly and without any issues, she returns her attention to me.

"Well *I* could've done it *with light*," I say, smiling, trying my best to be less grouchy. "No challenge in that."

She smiles, but only briefly. "You okay? How're you feeling?"

I shake my head. "Not great."

"Tell me."

I spit out a list of my symptoms.

"When is the last time you've eaten or had something to drink?" she asks. "I think you need something besides water. I bet your head hurts from not having any caffeine."

"What time is it?" I ask. "I'll eat when we meet Carla."

"Little after nine," she says. "When are we—"

"*Nine*?" I say, my voice rising. "I told you to wake me up by five so we could meet Carla for dinner."

She shakes her head. "You didn't say anything about that. Could it have been a dream you were having?"

Did I really fail to tell her?

"No. Are you sure? I thought I told you to wake me up by five."

"You told me to wake you but not why," she says.

Had I really forgotten to tell her why I needed to be up by five?

"Reggie called to check on you and told me to let you sleep, there was nothing else you needed to do today."

"*Shit.*"

"I'm sure Carla will understand," she says. "You've been—"

"That's all she's done is understand," I say, and I can tell my tone is too sharp, too biting. "I've let her down so much lately. I —" I reach for my phone to call Carla, but it hasn't charged enough to have cycled back on. "*Damn it.*"

"I'll call her," she says.

"She's got a new number. I'll have to wait until my phone comes back on. I've been so absent from her life I didn't even know she had a new number."

"Okay, listen. Drink the rest of your water. When your phone comes back on, call her. I'm going to fix you some food and get you something with caffeine in it. Do you want some aspirin too?"

I nod, which hurts. "Thanks. Yes, please. Sorry for being so ill."

"You're just dazed and exhausted."

"That's no excuse. Thank you for responding the way you have and for helping me. I really am sorry."

"My guess is you're far sorrier than you need to be," she says. "Forget it. It's no big deal. Drink your water. Call Carla. I'll be back in a few with something to eat."

L ater, after eating, showering, and spending some time with the girls, Anna and I are driving to Pottersville for a late supper with Carla.

Back at home, Dad and Verna are in negotiations with the girls over a variety of issues—including what video to watch, what snack to eat, and what constitutes something as arbitrary as a bedtime.

"You feeling better?" Anna asks.

I nod. "Some," I say. "Thank you."

I reach over and take her hand, holding and caressing it on the console between us.

We're driving down a two-lane rural highway, the moon high in the sky before us. On either side of the car flat wood forests of pine and oak and magnolias extend into visual infinity, their dark shapes growing darker and darker into the density.

"I spoke to Sam while you were sleeping," she says. "Just called to check on them."

Sam and Daniel, friends of ours recovering from severe trauma, had recently moved back to Tallahassee in an attempt to resume their lives. Before that, they had lived with or close to us and were a big part of our friend circle. Sam was an FDLE agent when she had been shot in the head, and now that she had mostly recovered—quite surprisingly and perhaps even miraculously—she is attempting to be an FDLE agent again. Daniel is a retired religion professor who hosts a true crime podcast with Merrick McKnight—Reggie's significant other.

"How is she? How's it going for her being back?"

"She says she's moving at half speed and everyone is letting her. Sounds like it's not easy, going about how she expected. Daniel's taking very good care of her. But the most interesting thing out of the entire conversation . . ."

"Yeah?"

"She says to be very careful with Tony Ford. Says he's not a team player, that he's always looking for an angle, angling for advancement."

"Good to know," I say, and then we are quiet for a beat.

"This is nice," Anna says. "Just the two of us like this."

"Yes it is," I say. "I've missed you. I always miss you when we're apart for any length of time at all."

We are in her Mustang. I am driving. The radio or a CD is playing very softly in the background, a barely audible acoustic folk serenade.

"Why does it seem like it's been so long since I felt like this?" she says. "We've been alone recent—Oh, I know. This is the first time in a very long time that we can be away from our girls without wondering what Chris might try."

I nod. She's right. I also feel more free, have more calm and clarity without the background static of worrying about my family's safety.

Chris has been a virus infecting our lives for so long that it will take a while to get all the poison out of our system, but we're already feeling the first freeing effects of what it will be like.

"I'm so relieved he's out of our lives permanently," she says. "We owe whoever did it more than we can ever pay."

I don't say anything.

"Any idea who that is yet?" she asks.

I shake my head. "No. And as much as it's most likely someone we know, I hope it isn't."

"Why?" she says. "Apart for the obvious reasons."

"The prolonged brutality of his murder," I say. "It wasn't an execution like the young woman we found. It was vicious extended torture."

"You can't understand someone we know wanting to do that to him?" she asks. "You didn't want to do it yourself?"

"I'm not saying that. The line between wanting to and doing it may seem fine, but it's not. It's an enormous gulf and a whole world between it."

"He deserved far more than what he got," she says.

"No one deserves what happened to him."

"Really? The man who tried to have you and your wife killed. The man whose actions led to your wife being beaten while she was pregnant, causing great damage and almost killing her baby? The man who broke into our home and held a gun to our little girl's head? He doesn't deserve the few minutes or hours of suffering he received?"

"I don't think Hitler or Bin Laden or Bundy or Wayne Williams deserved torture," I say. "I don't believe in torture. I don't think any good comes from it. I think it does great harm to the person doing the torturing."

"We're gonna have to agree to disagree on this," she says.

I can hear in her voice that she is growing angry.

I start to say something but she keeps talking. "You might see it differently if you were a woman. If you were more vulnerable than you are. Or were aware of it."

"Oh, so the issue is my lack of self-awareness?"

"That's not what I said, John."

She releases my hand and shifts in her seat so she's facing me, and I wonder if the movement in her seat was just to cover the fact that she wanted to let go of my hand.

"Run it back," I say. "I think it is. Are you mad at me about something?"

"Like what?"

"Do you think I should have been the one to torture and kill Chris?" I ask. "Did I fail to adequately protect and defend my family? Do you blame me for what happened, for what Chris did, for not stopping him sooner?"

"Those sound like thoughts you've had," she says. "Doesn't resemble anything I've said."

"Well, you seem mad at me and it seems like it's over far more than a philosophical disagreement about torture."

"I didn't think I was mad," she says. "At you or anyone else. I think I remember commenting on feeling good for the first time in a long time, but evidently I am."

"I am too."

Even after his death Chris is still causing problems for us, still here sowing discord and strife.

"You don't think I wanted to hack Chris into little pieces with a dull knife?" I ask. "Kill him with my bare hands? You don't think I wouldn't relish the thought of punching him repeatedly until he was unrecognizable?"

"I don't know."

"Wanting to do something and actually doing it are worlds apart," I say. "I haven't spent my life bringing people to justice who wanted to kill, only those who did."

"Think about that word—*justice*—I'd say that's what Chris got, what his punisher brought about."

I don't say anything.

"You don't think it was?" she asks, her tone sharp and challenging.

"I question what justice is," I say. "And I wonder if I've ever truly brought any about. Maybe it's an illusion like most everything else. But . . . think about it . . . you're asking someone who has spent a great deal of his life trying to catch murderers to say murder is okay. I can't do that. I *can* say I understand the murderous impulse, that I've seen it in myself, but I can't ever say murder is justifiable."

"You've killed people," she says.

"First of all I'm not trying to justify anything I've ever done, but I didn't say killing in self-defense or to protect another person. I said *murder*—the willful act of taking the life of another."

"Surely you're not saying you've never done that," she says.

"No, I'm not saying that at all. You know better. But again I'm not saying murder is wrong because I've never committed it. I don't base my belief about what's right and wrong on what I have or haven't done. This isn't about me."

"Of course it is," she says. "It's about all of us. You and me.

Our family and friends. And how you handle this case is going to have a huge impact on all of us."

She's right. She's absolutely right about that.

"Do you think I'd tell you if I killed Chris?" she asks.

"I'd say it's less likely after this conversation," I say with a smile and take her hand again. "I would hope so, but . . . I'd understand if you didn't. Given who you are, the way you love and look out for me, I could see you not telling me for my sake as much as your own."

"Earlier when I said I was mad," she says, "I wasn't saying I was mad at you. I'm mad. But not at you."

"I'm not mad at you," I say. "And I don't expect you to agree with me or see things the way I do."

"Good. 'Cause I don't."

"Never thought you did."

"Is that the most heated exchange we've ever had?" she asks.

I shake my head. "Not by a long shot."

"I mean since we've been a couple."

"Maybe."

"We okay?"

"Of course."

"I blame this on Chris," she says.

"Me too. I blame everything on that rat bastard."

She laughs. "See? Aren't you glad somebody tortured and killed him?"

"Never said I wasn't. Just that that part of me isn't going to stop the other part of me from trying to find out who it was and bearing witness against them."

"Even if it's your wife, best friend, or a member of your own family?"

15

L ike Pottersville itself, Rudy's Diner is exactly the same as it was when I was here last—except dingier, dirtier, more worn and faded, and even sadder somehow.

We pull off the empty highway into the oyster shell parking lot, take a moment to find more equilibrium than we've had on the drive over, then go inside.

As usual Carla is alone, seated at the counter near the register, but instead of school books, she's looking at her phone.

Rudy's looks like what it is—a closed down Waffle Shoppe reopened by an individual, the kitchen visible behind the counter, booths lining the windowed walls.

After greeting Carla and a few moments of awkward small talk, I walk over to the booth I used to think of as my own out of habit, the two women trailing after me.

"I'll make y'all anything you want," Carla said. "What would you like?"

"I told you," I said, "we're taking you to dinner. We didn't come here for you to work. We came to see you. Have a seat."

As she sits down across from us, Anna and I begin to pull

plastic storage containers of food out of the canvas bags we carried in.

"We brought dinner so you could sit here and enjoy it with us instead of having to cook," Anna says.

"Oh, sweet," Carla says. "That's awesome. Thank y'all so much."

"John remembered some of your favorite foods so I whipped them up for you," Anna says. "I just hope pregnancy hasn't changed your taste buds yet."

"Not so far, no. Just increased my appetite. These days I eat like an NFL lineman. Seems like all I do is eat."

As Anna spreads out the feast she has prepared and brought, I study Carla.

It hurts and angers me to see her still stuck in this dilapidated roadside diner. I had hoped after high school she would attend college—preferably somewhere far away from here. She had the grades and the desire. What had happened? Was it simply that I wasn't here to support her, to make sure she had what she needed, to insist she got at least a chance at a better life than the one she found herself in?

"So," Anna says, "catch us up on all things you. What's new? How's school?"

"School," she says with a sigh. "I attended one semester at Gulf Coast, but it was just too much with trying to keep this place open, so . . . I switched to online classes . . . which . . . were going great until I went and got myself knocked up. Right now I'm taking a little time off until after I have the baby, then I hope to be able to start back."

What are the chances of that? I wondered. As hard as her life is now, it will grow exponentially more difficult and challenging with a baby.

"When are you due?" Anna asks.

"You ready for this? Halloween. How about that?"

"Nothing wrong with that," I say. "One of my favorite holidays."

"John," Anna says, "will you bless the food so the pregnant woman doesn't have to wait any longer to eat?"

I do.

We eat in silence for a few moments. The food is extremely good, and I'm amazed both at how quickly Anna had prepared it and how she had managed to keep it hot and fresh from our kitchen in Wewa to this table inside of the dim diner outside of Pottersville.

"This is *so* good," Carla says. "Best meal I've had in a—I can't remember the last time I had something this good."

"It *is* great," I say. "Thank you."

"My pleasure," Anna says. "Glad y'all like it. I loved cooking it for y'all."

My mind drifts back to the crime scenes from this morning and think about both Chris and the as-yet unidentified young woman who must have been about Carla's age. I think about the ways in which they were killed, how their bodies were displayed or disposed of, and what that says about their killer or killers.

"Have you figured out where and how you're going to live and childcare and things like that?" Anna asks.

Carla shrugs. "Not really. Not totally anyway. I'm working on it though."

"Is the father involved and or going to be?"

She shakes her head and frowns, a single tear rolling down her right cheek. "No . . . and that's not a bad thing necessarily. The thing is . . . I was seeing someone and . . . it was going really well, but then he moved and we tried the long distance thing for a while but . . . And then . . . I was so stupid, but I was just so sad and so fuckin' lonely that I . . . and I wound up pregnant. And now the guy I was seeing—a really good guy who reminds me of John—is moving back early next year and . . ."

"Does he know you're pregnant?" I ask.

She shakes her head again. "No. I just haven't been able to tell him. The thing is . . . he really is an incredible guy and I think he's the one, that I could really be happy. He wants me to finish school and get a good job and get away from here. He lived in Tallahassee before he moved and that's where he's coming back to. The thing is . . . I wondered if you two would consider adopting my baby."

Anna and I are both speechless.

"I know. I know. So many couples out there want a baby and can't have one, but adoption is scary and not easy and . . . I even thought about going a more direct route, you know do it more unofficially. People do all the time. But all of it is just so . . . It's too much. And then you don't know who you're gonna get, I mean like what kind of parents the people will be. With you two I know my baby would be the luckiest baby in the entire world. I know it's a lot to ask and I don't expect an answer tonight, but would you just think about it? Talk to each other and pray about it and let me know later? Just don't tell me tonight—especially if the answer is *no*. I just couldn't take that right now."

16

"Did you know that was coming?" Anna asks.

We are back in her car on our way back home.

"No idea."

"Were you as shocked as I was?"

"Far more so I'm sure," I say. "I was floored."

"What was your initial reaction?" she asks.

"Honestly," I say, "I wanted to do it. Doesn't mean I think we should or that we even can or—but my initial response was a *yes*."

"Mine too."

"Really?"

"Really. And unlike you I don't feel guilty where she's concerned or responsible for her in some way and it was still a *yes*."

I consider whether my response was out of obligation or guilt.

"I resisted the temptation to ask," she adds, "because I'd be happy with anything, but . . . what if it's a boy. I'd be happy with a third girl, but . . . what if it was our first boy?"

I smile. She's getting way, way ahead of everything, but I

don't say anything. I have no desire to dampen her excitement at the possibility of adding to our family.

We still have a lot to think about and consider, including what will happen and how we'll feel if Carla changes her mind —now or later—but we'll save all that for another time.

"It's just . . ." she begins. "I mean . . . with Chris out of our lives and the possibility of a new baby coming into our lives . . . I just feel so hopeful, so . . . happy."

Chris isn't out of our lives. Not yet. And I don't just mean the investigation and all its implications but the heated conversation we had on the way over to see Carla, but again I keep my own counsel.

"Speaking of Chris," I say, "Darlene and an FDLE agent named Ford are going to want to interview you this week."

She doesn't say anything.

"Have you thought about what you'll tell them?" I ask.

She shrugs. "That I woke up with a sense of foreboding. That I went through what had become a typical day lately— mostly trying to protect my daughters from a murdering, stalking, unhinged man while trying to make them feel safe and give them a sense of normalcy."

"Might not want to stress that part so much."

"How about how happy I am that he's dead?"

"You can say whatever you want to," I say, "but the more of that kind of talk there is the more and harder they're going to not only look at you, but me and our friends and family."

"Gotcha," she says. "Well, I don't want to draw any extra attention to anyone—especially the person who actually did it."

"They're going to ask you to take them through your day and your whereabouts during the estimated time of death."

"Which is?"

"Ten and three I think," I say. "They may have it narrowed down even more by the time they talk to you. When did you go to the park?"

"It was pretty late," she says. "I was missing you and going a little stir crazy being cooped up in the house so much. Girls were too. So even though they had already had their baths and dinner, I decided to take them to the state park—I mean the campgrounds, recreational area, whatever they call it now. I asked Merrill. He said absolutely nothing would happen to us and I believed him."

"Did he go with you?"

"He went, but not with us. Told me he'd be there, watching, protecting, but that I wouldn't see him. Just to enjoy ourselves and not worry. So we did—enjoy ourselves, I mean. And not worry too. We did both. It was nice. We stopped by the Dollar Store on the way up and got ice cream and took it with us. We played on the jungle gym, slid on the slides. I pushed them in the swings. It was really nice."

"Did you see Merrill?"

She shakes her head. "But I knew he was there."

"How about Chris?" I ask.

"Same thing. Never saw him, but knew he was there."

"Did Merrill?"

"I'm sure. I mean, if I did . . . But I'm not going to tell anyone else that. Won't even tell them he was there. Should I not tell you either? I know you have a dual role in all this. You're sort of working Chris's case too, right? Would it be better if I didn't tell you everything?"

I shake my head. "No," I say. "I can't imagine that would be better in any way."

"Okay," she says.

"You said you went late. How late?"

"Meant later than we usually do. We were there from around seven until eight."

"Then what?"

"Went home. Baths. Stories. Snacks. Bed."

"I thought you had already bathed them?"

"Did it again," she says. "They got sweaty and sticky at the park."

"And you didn't leave the house again?"

"You askin' as you or as an investigator?"

"I hate that you have to ask that," I say. "You know I'm always both."

"Even with your wife?"

"Of course not."

She laughs. "You couldn't not be an investigator if you wanted to—not even for a moment—and you don't really want to anyway. Which is why I'd like to stop talking about this for tonight. I was so happy just a few moments ago. Can we go back to baby talk? I mean, given our fight on the drive over and the stress of today—and all the recent days leading up to it . . . I'm just so tired. I promise I'll tell you everything if you really want me to."

"I'll ask you just one more question tonight," I say. "Have you already started thinking about boys names?"

She lets out a huge laugh that is both a reaction to my question and a release of tension.

"Years ago," she says. "Years ago. And I'll tell you the truth . . . it's very common, but I'm awfully partial to the name *John*."

17

"How hard do you think Reggie's gonna push to solve Chris's murder?" Dad asks.

He and I are standing out in my front yard, while inside the house Anna and Verna are discussing decorations and activities for Johanna's upcoming birthday party.

"She left Darlene on it. She's relentless. And she asked for an FDLE agent so there's oversight and accountability."

He nods to himself and seems to think about it.

When he runs a thumbnail along the gray stubble along his jawline I can see the knuckles of his right hand are bruised and swollen.

"She doesn't want anyone to be able to say we did it and covered it up," I add.

"And if we did?"

"Then it won't be covered up."

He twists his lips down into a frown and seems to think about that too.

"It doesn't necessarily have to be one of us," he says. "I'm sure Chris was mixed up in all kind of criminal activities—before he was arrested the first time and since."

"We'll look into that too."

"So you're gonna be involved?"

I nod.

"That's good," he says. "That's good."

"Officially I'll be working the murder of the young woman, but unofficially..."

The night is hot and humid, the air thick and still and moist. The bright moon casts faint shadows and shimmers on the unmoving surface of Julia's face. From down by the lake a loud cacophony of crickets and frogs and other nocturnal critters drowns out all the other sounds save our voices.

"A lot of people owe you," he says. "Could've easily been one of them."

Sylvia, Reggie's mother comes to mind as do Daniel and Sam and others—including Verna, Dad's new wife.

"I'm thinking even if one of them didn't do it," he adds, "they might confess to it if they thought you or Anna did."

I haven't thought of that. He could be right. Actually, he could be considering doing it if it comes to that.

Did he punch a wall to bruise and swell his knuckles to setup a future confession if it looks like his son or daughter in-law are going to be charged in the case?

"What about Randa Raffield?" he says. "She said she was going to do it. Maybe she did."

"We'll look at her hard," I say, "though it's hard to see how she could've done it."

"Be nice if she did somehow," he says. "She's already in custody. Probably going to spend a lot of time in prison anyway. Lot easier for one person to serve the same time for two different crimes than ruining two different lives."

I've never heard Dad talk quite like this before. He sounds less like a lifelong lawman than a few ex-cons I know.

"Wish this would've happened in Pottersville a couple of years back," he says.

I think about the advantages and disadvantages of that. If it appears a local agency is corrupt or covering something up—even in a single investigation—the governor can task FDLE with investigating both the crime and the coverup. Something far worse than inviting an agent in to assist with the investigation in the first place. Reggie is being smart and she knows it.

"You sound different now than when you were in office," I say. "Or maybe it's just different about this particular case."

"Maybe. Maybe not. I've just seen so much over the years and . . . know that justice is at best a very elusive concept."

"I don't disagree," I say, "but doesn't that mean we have to be even more careful not to apply what we do arbitrarily?"

"You've always been more idealistic than me," he says.

Is that what it comes down to? Idealism versus realism or even nihilism.

"Did you ever intentionally not solve a case?" I ask.

He nods. "Of course. Remember Miss Iris?"

I nod.

"She killed her husband," he says. "But only after years of him battering her. Something like that . . . I wasn't going to take the chance that a jury would acquit her. Juries are unpredictable and too often stupid. Another time I did it was when a teen killed the man who molested him as a kid. Unsolveds aren't always bad. And sometimes the colder a case is . . . the better."

In some ways he's talking about a very different era than the one we're living in now, but in others things haven't changed as much as they seem to have.

"Remember the first night he showed up over here?" Dad says. "I knew then it was going to end up something like this. I just wanted it to be him instead of you or your wife or girls—or even one of us. Then when he broke into your home and held a gun on you, on Johanna . . ."

I let that one hang in the atmosphere between us.

"Man like that . . . that would do that . . . not gonna stop, never gonna change. Only thing for them is to be put down like a rabid dog. Been better for everyone if it had been done sooner, but . . . got there eventually."

Jack

D riving home from John's with Verna, after spending time with his granddaughters, he thinks about the threat Chris has posed to his family and how hard it had been for him not to put him down sooner.

Jack Jordan is or at least was, for most of his life, an old school, small town, Deep South sheriff—something that's about as all-powerful as an American citizen can get. Or at least it used to be. He's accustomed to doing things a certain way. His way.

To the best of his ability to recollect and to evaluate such matters, he doesn't think he ever abused or misused his power. At least not in any meaningful way. He had never taken any kind of kickback, never played politics, never allowed favors from rich or poor, powerful or powerless. But he had also never felt the need to strictly color within the lines when common sense and good judgement dictated otherwise.

He still felt guilty for how he had handled John's transition from submissive teenage son to young man making his own way in the world. Was still trying to make it up to him every chance he got.

He had not supported John's move to Atlanta, his spiritual pursuits, his inexplicable need to be a minister and an investigator. It had been among other things a failure of imagination on his part—that and stubbornness and pride. He full well expected John to fail, to come back home and ask his dad for a job as an investigator in the Pottersville Sheriff's department.

But it wasn't just that he didn't support him, he actually abandoned him, acted as if John had betrayed him somehow. During that time Frank Morgan had been far more a father to John than he had. Of course what frightens and shames him even more is he might still be.

That's why he knew he couldn't allow a piece of shit like Chris Taunton to try to kill his son, to stalk and threaten his family, to actually break into their home and hold a gun to his granddaughter's little head without doing something about it.

There's nothing he wouldn't do for his son. He and Verna are alike in that.

He thinks about what she had done for her own son and concludes she would understand what he had done for his.

He tries to push away such thoughts, but it's all he can think about now.

He wants to talk to her about it, but he's not going to put that on her. It wouldn't be fair, wouldn't be right. And that's something he's going to do. Whether it agrees with or contradicts the law, Jack Jordan is going to do what he thinks is right.

18

After Dad and Verna leave, I sit down in one of the outdoor metal chairs beneath the pergola on the side of our house and call the jail administrator back.

I had expected to hear from him earlier in the day, and it worries me that I haven't.

The Gulf County jail is not part of the sheriff's department. It is owned and operated by the board of county commissioners and is run by an administrator hired by the board to do so.

Though the guards are certified like state correctional officers, the security of the jail is lax and laid back to an extreme that makes all of us in the sheriff's department perpetually uneasy. For most of those arrested in our small county—on charges like violation of probation, DUIs, various drug charges—it's not much of an issue, but for someone like Randa Raffield it's a huge problem—something we warned the jailer about.

Unlike the prison where I work part-time, the jail has no sallyport, no dual locking doors with a holding area between them. A single door separates the inmates from freedom—and it is often not secured like it should be. We routinely observe it open, one of the inmate cooks, hanging out of it smoking, as we come and go from the sheriff's department.

Though the jail has a few two-person cells and a holding cell up front, the vast majority of inmates are in an open bay dorm in the back.

Recently, an inmate in one of the cells was able to climb up through the ceiling, across the catwalk into the courthouse, and down into the judge's office to use his computer. Supposedly that's not possible any longer, but with an old jail built in the 1960s run the way this one is, there's no telling what other security breaches there are just waiting for someone like Randa to exploit.

Fortunately, female inmates are housed at the Liberty County jail, which has far tighter security procedures in place, but even Gulf County's female inmates pass through the Gulf County jail on their way to and from court. They're housed in a special holding cell up front designated to do so.

Patch McMyers, the jail administrator, doesn't answer until the fifth ring.

"John, sorry I didn't get back with you today," he says, his voice sounding dry and sleepy. "I've still got a few details to track down."

"Is there an issue?" I ask. "Should've just been a simple verification, right?"

"Well . . . yeah, but I wanted to be absolutely sure about everything, be able to say with certainty where the inmate was at all times."

"And you're not able to so far?"

"We're almost there," he says. "Just crossing t's and dotting i's."

"Have you verified she's still in custody?" I ask.

"Yes," he says. "I had a correctional officer not only put eyes on her earlier today, but actually physically touch her and take her fingerprints."

"And you confirmed it was her?"

"Sure did. So we're all good there."

"So what's the problem?"

"Verifying her exact whereabouts at the time the murder was committed."

"You haven't been able to do that yet?" I ask. "What's the holdup?"

"Well, she was actually up here in our jail at the time—or on her way, depending on what time the murder took place."

"Really? Why?"

"She had a court appearance first thing the next morning and the Liberty County jail was going to be shorthanded the next day, so they asked if they could bring her the night before and have her stay in the holding cell overnight?"

"And that's what she did?"

"Seems so. There're a few little anomalies with the paperwork I wanted to clear up before I called you back. Should have them straightened out before long. I'll call you as soon as I have everything in order and know for certainty."

"But at this point you believe Randa Raffield was in a Gulf County jail holding cell when the murder took place?" I ask.

"Most likely yes—there or on her way to it."

The route between Liberty County and Gulf County jails takes Randa directly by the Dead Lakes Campgrounds where Chris was murdered. Whether she was en route or in the holding cell, she can't be ruled out as a prime suspect.

I'm sitting thinking about that when Anna opens the door.

"Everything okay?" she asks.

"Guess it depends on how you look at it," I say and tell her what Patch McMyers has just told me.

"So it's at least possible Randa could've done it?" she says. "How is that anything but great news?"

"Just makes the investigation more complicated," I say.

"Exactly."

"If she didn't do it, it's the kind of thing a defense attorney can use to sow seeds of reasonable doubt."

"Exactly," she says. "Like I said, I don't see how this is anything but really good news."

19

D ays pass while we wait for autopsy results and work to gather more information.

We compile witness statements, chase down leads, catalog evidence, and coordinate the various activities each of us is undertaking.

Once an investigation gathers momentum it can speed along with a great deal of velocity, but getting it to that point, actually getting it moving at all in the early stages can take a while and requires a tremendous amount of both energy and patience.

On the third day since the bodies were discovered we have gathered into Reggie's office for a conference call with the ME.

Her office is not exactly small, but it wasn't designed to accommodate so many people—me, Arnie Ward, Darlene Weatherly, Tony Ford, and Jessica Young—so it feels crowded and a little awkward.

From what we can tell so far, it appears the murders aren't connected, but rather than going over them separately and only including the investigators working that case in the calls,

Reggie has summoned us all in and is going to have the ME go over both preliminary autopsies at the same time. And though she hasn't said so explicitly, my guess is she's doing it in this manner as a way of allowing me to hear the evidence associated with Chris's murder.

The call comes and after a few formalities and a little small talk, we jump into the exchange of information we as investigators most need.

"Which one do you want to start with?" Hanlon asks.

"Let's take them in the order they were discovered," Reggie says.

She's doing this to ensure I'll get to hear everything he says about Chris, and I wonder if it's obvious to the others, especially Ford.

"I know you all know this," Hanlon says, "but I'm going to remind you anyway because it's important that you remember. The results I'm sharing with you are very preliminary and are still subject to change. Please don't forget that."

"Got it," Reggie says. "And I'll remind them often."

"Don't have a lot to add to what I told you at the scene," Hanlon says. "Preliminary autopsy results confirmed most of what I felt comfortable enough hypothesizing initially. The victim underwent a significant amount of trauma over three distinct periods. The majority of the blunt force trauma—the assault, the beating—was antemortem. We were able to confirm that the bat found in the woods near the scene did contain the victim's blood and is consistent with some of the wounds found on the body. But not all of them. Hands and fists were used as well as another tool—a hammer or mallet of some kind. As I suspected, the stab wounds were inflicted post mortem and there were twelve of them and they were made with the weapon that was left inside the victim."

"Which we've confirmed came from HC's RV that was

broken into," Reggie says. "That, the phone used to call dispatch, the pillowcase used for the hood, and the rope used to cinch it around the neck."

It's significant the killer didn't come to the park prepared to do what he did, but we've already covered that so no one brings it up again now.

"According to HC," Ford says, "that's all that's missing, so the bat and the hammer or whatever the other implement used was came from somewhere else."

Perhaps the killer did bring some of what he needed but not everything. Or maybe he stole those other items from a different location in the park. Or perhaps he didn't bring them at all because he's staying in the park.

"So given all that," Darlene says, speaking in the general direction of the speaker phone, "what's the cause of death?"

"Afraid I don't have one yet. We're gonna have to wait until we get all the results back—particularly toxicology."

"Tox takes time," Ford says.

He's right. It can take weeks for the toxicology test results to be completed.

"Can you give us anything to work with in the meantime?" Ford continues. "Even if it's subject to change later?"

Darlene says, "I figured it was down to blunt force trauma or blood loss since the stab wounds happened post mortem."

"It could be, but our findings don't lead us to be able to definitively conclude that it has to be one of them. He suffered a lot of trauma and he lost a lot of blood, and either one of them may be what led to his death—probably did—but until I have all the information and since there's nothing absolutely convincing that it was one or the other . . . I'm going to leave cause of death as *undetermined* for now."

"We understand," Reggie says. "How about time of death? Were you able to narrow it down any?"

"Unfortunately not. There were no stomach contents to go on. It had been a while since he had eaten. So same range—ten to three."

"Anything else?" Reggie asks.

"Think that's it for now."

"Okay, how about the female victim?"

"Biggest thing to tell you is we still have no ID. We rolled the prints. Sent them to FDLE. They've searched both state and national databases . . . and nothing. This young woman has never been printed before. So we're gonna have to ID her in a different way."

Our best bet will be by searching through missing persons until we get a match, then using DNA to confirm. Usually we use something like the missing person's hairbrush to pull DNA from. If we can find nothing with her DNA on it, we can use a parent if we have to. All of which takes time.

It's gonna take time . . . A whole lot of precious time.

Random and unbidden the line from the George Harrison song pops into my mind and I'm taken back to the old rented farm house where Susan and I lived for a time on Flakes Mill Road in Atlanta and waking up to it back when I first began working on the Stone Cold Killer case.

"We'll have DNA ready for when you have a possible match," Hanlon is saying. "We'll also have a way to match ballistics when you locate a murder weapon. We removed a .38 caliber projectile from inside her skull. She was shot in the back of the head but it wasn't at pointblank range. Bullet is in pretty good shape."

"That'll help us nail him," Arnie says. "That's great."

"I'd say she is on the younger end of the spectrum I gave you at the scene. Probably between sixteen and nineteen. She was in good health, took good care of herself. No signs of injuries or surgical procedures. Not a lot for you to go on except

. . . some scarring on the backside of the pubic ramus bone indicates she has given birth, which could be connected to a tattoo on the top of her left foot—the only tattoo she has. It's of an infant's footprint and has the name *Brandon* above it."

20

"Usually if someone pulls into the park," Evelyn Hillman says, "they either stop over by the picnic and play area, or they drive all the way through—you know, like make the circle. If they're just riding around. It's what the deputy does."

She is an extremely thin older woman with long, coarse gray hair, sunbaked skin, and the deep, gurgly, phlegmy voice of a lifelong chain smoker who has lived a very long life. She is wearing white shorts and a bikini top that reveals saggy, deeply wrinkled skin and far too much of her small, shriveled, pointy breasts.

We are standing near her Cruiser Aire fifth wheel camper trailer on the backside of the Dead Lakes Campground.

Not only is her campsite the last in line, so it is nearest the pond and has the best view of the crime scene, but according to HC, she is the guest who pays the most attention to what's going on in the park and what everybody else is doing.

"How often do you see a deputy drive through?" I ask.

"Usually about twice a day—once in the afternoon and once in the evening. Tell you who does it the most is Deputy Faircloth."

Everywhere we turn there is Cody Faircloth.

"But like I said," she continues, "that night was different. Lots of cars coming and going, but they didn't park by the playground and get out, and they didn't drive all the way through. They stayed mostly over there in that field where the body was found."

"Different cars?"

"Different cars. Different times."

"Do you remember any of the vehicles?"

"There was a Mustang. Know the headlights cause I used to have one myself. Should've never sold that car. Miss it. But it couldn't pull this baby," she adds as she reaches out and tenderly caresses her camper.

Anna drives a Mustang.

"Also saw a little truck—like a Toyota or an old Datsun or something—and a black BMW," she says.

Merrill drives a black BMW.

He and Anna were both here that day, but earlier than the estimated time of death.

"Do you remember if that was earlier in the evening or later?"

"Not sure. Maybe both. Seems like I seen them twice, but can't be positive. It was all very suspicious, so I called the cops."

"You did?" I ask in surprise. This is the first time I've heard of this, though I had read the notes from her initial interview.

"I certainly did," she says. "This is our home—those of us who live here, even if for a short while—can't have loitering or drug dealing or lover's lane here. By the time Deputy Faircloth arrived, they were gone. He looked around to see what was going on over there, was thorough, took a while, but told me he didn't see anything and for me just to call back if they show up again and he'd come a runnin'."

"How did he tell you that?" I ask.

"Huh?"

"Did you walk over there and hangout with him while he did his search or—"

"He come over here and talked to me and HC when he was done."

"Have you remembered anything else suspicious or out of the ordinary from that night?" I ask.

She shakes her head.

"Do you know if anyone is missing anything, had anything stolen recently?"

"Just HC. His spare camper was broken into."

"No one else?"

"No. And I would know. I'm sort of the unofficial head of the neighborhood watch."

I know the futility of my next question, but I ask it anyway.

"How about between eight and twelve weeks ago," I say, "remember anything suspicious or out of the ordinary?"

She looks up into the branches of the tall pines scattered around us and squints and wrinkles up her face as if trying to access a memory from an ancient, failing hard drive in need of defragging.

"I mean . . . there are always little things here and there, but nothing stands out."

"What kinds of little things?"

"We get the occasional crazies, the homeless, teens throwing a party in the woods," she says. "From time to time we've had a recently released child molester come up and pretend he was having a picnic, but he was right over there near the playground just a-staring at the youngins on the playground."

"Do you remember seeing a young woman in her late teens with long, thick black hair?"

"If she had the biggest bluest saddest eyes you've ever seen I do. Stood out because she was so striking. You don't usually see *black* black hair like that with blues eyes. If I'm remembering right, the girl I'm thinking of was with her folks. Seems like they were in one of them big old Cadillacs. I don't know . . . Seemed sort of odd. Think they were just here for a few hours, like just having a family picnic or something. Stayed over there under that first pavilion the whole time. Seems like they had a little boy and a baby with 'em. But I could be mixing all this up."

"Did they hike the nature trails or walk into the woods behind the field where HC has his extra camper parked?" I ask.

She shrugs her boney shoulders, her chest caving in some, her small, shriveled breasts threatening to slide out of the tiny triangles of bathing suit fabric across them.

"Maybe," she says. "Seems so. Can't be sure."

"Did you see anyone from here talking to them?"

"Let's see . . . Not for any length of time. I think this was before HC and Georgia got here, so Fred Spears would've been the host at that time. I think. But . . . Fred wasn't as nice or friendly as HC, so he probably didn't . . . But it does seem like somebody did . . . you know, I think it was Captain Jack."

21

When I knock on the door of the older model Jayco Jay Flight travel trailer, Captain Jack opens the door right away and, instead of inviting me in, quickly steps out and closes the door behind him.

I actually have to step off the side of the small portable steps to keep from having to charge him with assault on a law enforcement officer.

In all our dancing around, I notice he's wearing an ankle holster with a small weapon in it—most likely a .22, .38, or a small 9mm.

When we're both on ground level, I can see just how large a man Captain Jack actually is. At least six-six with massive, meaty hands and a lean, lanky build, he's muscular, especially for an older man.

Beneath a well-worn beige and brown Remington Firearms baseball cap, his squinty, beady eyes look wary and suspicious, but his mouth, which is surrounded by a gray Van Dyke, is smiling.

We introduce ourselves, and I tell him what Evelyn Hillman

said about him possibly talking to the family under the first pavilion.

"I don't remember them, I truly don't," he says. "But I go for a walk around the park at least twice a day, and I often strike up a little convo with anyone I encounter, so . . . it's a safe bet I did."

"But you don't remember them in particular?"

He shakes his large, long head. "Sorry."

"Remember seeing any black-haired, blue-eyed teenage girls around here between eight and twelve weeks go?"

He shrugs. "I'm gonna tell you the truth . . . I live the way I do—like out in the middle of nowhere —because I don't much care for people. So I don't usually notice them much. I speak, exchange a few pleasantries, and move on. I'm not gonna be much help in the details department."

"Same true for last Sunday night?" I say.

"Didn't see no black-haired, blue-eyed girl if that's what you mean."

"See or hear anything suspicious, out of the ordinary?"

"More traffic on the other side of the lake over there than usual, but that was about it."

"I notice you didn't give a statement the morning we did our initial interviews," I say. "Were you not here?"

"Monday morning . . . I was here. Must've sent a cop over here with a gentle knock. Didn't hear him. And I wasn't about to come poking my nose into anything that didn't concern me. Don't care for people much and, no offense, but that goes double for cops."

"I understand," I say. "I really do. How'd you get the name *Captain Jack*?"

He shakes his head and frowns dismissively. "Another life . . . back before I—"

He stops abruptly.

"Back before what?" I say.

"Look, you seem like a reasonably intelligent and decent guy, but I really just want to be left alone."

"Just give me enough so I can leave you alone," I say.

"That never works," he says, dropping his head for a moment and shaking it slowly. When he looks back up, his eyes lock with mine. "Don't make me regret this. Back before I started living off the grid, in my previous life, I was a police captain in a little town in Central Florida."

"So your dislike for cops is a form of self-loathing," I say.

He laughs out loud at that, his face transforming into a softer, younger version of itself, his eyes momentarily losing their disdain and distrust.

"Yeah," he says, "I guess in a way it is."

"What brings you to Wewa?"

"I go from campground to campground," he says. "A lot of us do. It's my way of touring this great state of ours."

"While living off the grid?"

"More or less. I'm not completely off, but I'm about as far off as you can be without being completely off. Hell, this little town here is practically off the grid."

I nod and smile. "Certainly is. So, your statement is you don't know anything, didn't see or hear anything, and you'd like to be left alone."

"Exactly right," he says.

"Okay," I say, "just need your full name for the statement and I'll leave you alone."

I want his name to do a background search on him. A former cop now living off the grid has to have an interesting backstory.

He knows what I'm doing and hesitates a moment.

"Tell you what," I say, "just let me see your driver's license and I'll copy it down from there."

"Don't have it on me," he says.

He's stalling and I know it and he knows I know it. Because

he's not suspected of a crime or even being a material witness at this point, I can't legally detain him or require he tell me who he is and produce his DL, but there are ways around it. He knows as well as I do that I can just get the tag number off the truck parked beside his camper. I could also get his information from HC. As a guest staying here he'll be registered. There are other ways too. But now I want to see how he'll handle my request and why he wants to remain anonymous.

"I don't mind waiting while you step inside and get it."

He shakes his head and smiles but there's no warmth in it. "You know I don't have to show it to you."

"I could just make you produce your concealed carry permit for the little piece you have strapped to your ankle," I say. "Make sure you're carrying it legally."

He slowly reaches into his back pocket and withdraws his wallet. Flipping it open, he holds it out for me to read.

"John Peter Patterson, Jr." I read. "Why does that sound so familiar?"

He shrugs. "Couldn't tell you. Is that all?"

"How about that concealed carry permit?"

He produces it. I examine it quickly and return it to him.

"Thank you for your cooperation, Captain Jack," I say. "Have a good day."

"You too, Investigator Jordan," he says. "And don't you be believing everything you read about me now, you hear?"

22

"You're tellin' me we've got a honest-to-goodness real life internet celebrity staying at our little campground?" Reggie says.

"We certainly do."

It's later that night. After dinner and playtime with the girls, Anna and I put them to bed and come into my library and begin Googling Captain Jack.

When I realize who he is I call Reggie.

John Patterson, Jr. is the author of *Wickedness in the Woods: Missing, Murdered, and Abducted in the Parks and Playgrounds of America.* He has a popular website, Youtube channel, and blog about what he sees as a conspiracy of silence about the countless people who go missing or are murdered in national and state parks, favorite camping sites, and hiking trails.

He's a popular figure with a huge following, and has appeared on both network and cable news shows and in documentaries on the subject.

As a former police officer he brings a certain credibility to his claims, which aren't without merit or statistical support—a credibility that is all but lost for many who first tune in to hear what he has to say when he posits the possibility of paranormal explanations.

"Why didn't you recognize him?" she asks. "You've seen him on TV, haven't you?"

"Anna asked me the same thing. He's a lot bigger in person. He was wearing a baseball cap pulled down low. And he's now sporting facial hair. In all the TV appearances and video and pictures online he's clean shaven."

"If you'd've just been a little more on your game, you could've recognized him and gotten his autograph," she says.

"My guess is he dresses differently, wears the cap, grows the Van Dyke, and goes by a different name when he's investigating," I say.

"What do you think he's here investigating?" she asks.

"With him it could be either of the murders or the Bigfoot sighting. Hard to know."

"That's right, someone did say they saw Bigfoot up there, didn't they? I had forgotten about that. We need to find out what he's up to."

"Yes, we do."

"And we will."

"Yes, we will."

"Did you get the emails I sent you?" she asks.

"Just about to read them now."

Tony and Darlene had driven to Tallahassee today to interview Chris's parents and two attorneys from the firm he used to work for. Tony had made audio recordings of the interviews and sent them to Reggie, who sent them to me.

"The dad—Lyle—is going to be a problem," she says. "He wouldn't even let Darlene in his house. Only Tony. He's convinced you killed Chris and our department is helping to cover it up. Says he plans to go to the press if FDLE doesn't arrest you soon. The mom seems to be more reasonable, but she has no influence over the dad and she's in bad shape.

Don't know how much longer she'll be with us. The partners in the law firm say what you'd expect. Chris played fast and loose with the law, clients' money, and ethics. Even before he was arrested or anything had come out about him, they had terminated him from the firm for a host of questionable behaviors, including complaints from secretaries and paralegals of sexual harassment. Oh, and we got Chris's phone log back."

I can tell by the way she says it there's something about it that's a problem for us. Chris's phone had yet to be found, but Verizon had provided a log of all his incoming and outgoing calls.

"Yeah?"

"He called Anna several times the day he was killed," she says.

"He used to do that all the time," I say, "but she blocked his number so I'm surprised it even shows up."

"It wouldn't if it was blocked," she says. "So it must not be. But that's not all. There's also a call from her phone to his within an hour of when we believe he was killed."

I feel like I've been sucker punched to the gut and can't get my breath.

"John?" she says. "You there?"

"Yeah. I'll look at the logs and talk to Anna about the calls," I say.

"I'm sure Tony and Darlene will bring it up when they interview her. Just wanted y'all to be prepared."

When I end the call with Reggie, I look over at Anna.

We are on the floor of my library, each with our laptops and various reports, notes, and witness statements scattered around.

She is concentrating on something on the screen of her laptop and it takes a moment for her to look up.

"What is it?" she says.

"I thought you blocked Chris's number from your phone," I say.

"I did," she says. "Several times. He kept getting different numbers—I think he was getting those prepaid burner phones—so I had to keep doing it. Why?"

"The call log from his phone shows several calls from his phone to yours and at least one from your phone to his."

"Okay."

"Close to the time he was murdered."

"Oh."

"Did you talk to him on Sunday evening?"

She doesn't respond right away.

"Tony and Darlene are going to ask you about them when they interview you," I say. "Reggie wanted you to know ahead of time so you could be prepared."

She nods slowly. "That's very nice of her."

"What will you tell them?"

"That he got a new number and started harassing me again. I didn't answer the calls but suspected it was him—he'd done it so many times before. Finally, I called him back to confirm it was him and to let him know I'd be blocking him so it was futile to keep calling back."

"What really happened?" I ask.

"That's all true," she says. "More or less. I just plan to leave out the parts where l threatened to kill him with my bare hands, things like that."

As we're talking, I pull up the call logs on my computer and glance through them.

"But . . . it wasn't a new phone," I say. "The log goes back quite a ways. I don't see any calls to or from you in a long time, then suddenly on the day he was murdered there are several."

"The truth is I unblocked him because I had some things I wanted to say to him," she says. "And if you think I need to tell them that, I will. I just thought it'd be easier not to get into all that."

"Why didn't you tell me?" I ask.

"I was going to—and then . . ."

"You've had plenty of time since then to mention it—not just that you called him but what you said, what he said."

"I'm sorry. I really had intended to and then in all the aftermath of everything and what Carla asked us . . . I forgot. I really did."

"What did you say to him?"

"I don't know, I just berated him. I just went off. I was so . . . mad at him. Just told him what a pathetic piece of shit he was, how he didn't deserve to have a precious little girl like Taylor, that she'd be better off if he were dead. That if he didn't leave us alone I was going to kill him myself, that nobody would care and I'd get away with it. That sort of thing."

"That was a very risky thing to do given how unstable he was."

"In the moment I didn't care. Or . . . actually I was hoping he'd make a move. I was just so . . . mad at him."

"I know. And I get it. What did he say?"

"I didn't really give him the chance to say anything. When I hung up I blocked him again."

I think about what she has said.

"I'm sorry, John," she says. "I'm sorry to have brought him into your life. I'm sorry for all this you're having to deal with. I'm sorry I unblocked him and called him. I'm sorry I didn't tell you. I'm so, so sorry for everything."

23

W ith Anna asleep beside me, I listen to the interview Tony Ford conducted with Lyle Taunton.

The room is dark and breezy and I have my earbuds turned up.

The girls are back in their room. Our door is open—as is theirs right across the hall. And a baby monitor sits beside the clock on Anna's bedside table.

"I'm not saying my son was perfect," Lyle is saying, "but he didn't deserve this. No one deserves something like that—'cept maybe a terrorist or child molester. And my son wasn't neither of those things. He was a human being with some issues, but he had really started putting his life back together."

"How so?" Tony asks.

"Before he fell from grace, he had very little to do with me and nothing to do with his mother. He was a high-powered, hotshot attorney and . . . to be honest . . . he was full of himself. He had made a lot of money. Had a reputation as one of the best criminal defense attorneys in town, so . . . yeah, he could be cocky. But being arrested, losing everything—especially his family—changed him. He wasn't the same person he used to be. He had humility. He was trying real hard to be a good man. His whole priorities changed. He didn't rush in and out anymore. He took time to . . . you know, listen and . . . care. It's the closest we had been in years. His mother and I were never going to get back together or anything like that, but . . . because of him, we could be civil to one another. He made us a kind of family again. He did that. That was all him. His mother's in bad shape. Has been for a long time. Had all kinds of surgeries—had to have both her knees replaced this past year. She lives in one of those assisted living apartments. Can't go anywhere. Can't do anything. He breathed new life into her. What little joy she's had this past year was because of Chris."

There's a break in the audio and it sounds like Lyle is drinking something.

"That's the thing that bothers me the most about this," he says. "Chris was killed right in the middle of turning his life around. He didn't get a chance to complete the process. No one got to see the new and improved version of him because he was beaten to death before they could. Son of a bitch thinks he can take my son from me like that and his buddies will cover up for him, well I'm not gonna let that happen. I meant what I said. You guys do your damn job and arrest Jordan or I'm gonna take y'all all down."

"Please give us time to conduct our investigation, Mr. Taunton," Tony says. "I assure you we're an outside, independent organization. We won't cover up for anyone and we'll shine a light on those who try to, but . . . you've got to give us time to gather evidence and make a case. We're gonna follow wherever the evidence leads—no matter where that may be."

When the first recording ends, I grab my phone off the nightstand, angling it away from Anna so the light won't bother her, and select the second recording—the one with Audrey Taunton, Chris's mother.

"Your husband said Chris was turning his life around," Tony says. "That you all were becoming a family again."

"We were allowed back into Chris's life a little, yes, but my ex-husband may have wanted that to mean more than it really did."

Unlike Lyle, I had never seen Audrey so I had no visual of her, but that didn't stop me from picturing her and Tony and Darlene and her little assisted living room. Based on her voice, I picture her as a well-educated and once-proud woman humbled by life and the ravages of time.

Lying here in the dark, listening to the audio recording, I'm imagining the scene and characters the way I would if I were listening to an old-time radio show or an audio book. There's something very intimate about having voices going directly into your head, especially in the dark, especially with earbuds. I've observed this before while listening to podcasts while trying unsuccessfully to fall asleep.

"How did you see it?" Darlene asks.

"Chris had lost everything and everyone," she says. "He needed us again, so . . . he reached out to reconnect. I was glad he did—no matter the reason. I was just happy to be in his life again."

"Do you think he was just using you?" Tony asks.

"No, not just, and that's what kids do, isn't it? That's what parents are for. I love my son. Would do anything for him. I just think I see him a bit more clearly, more honestly, than my ex-husband did."

"Did y'all give him money?" Darlene asks.

"Some. Neither of us has much, but I helped him as much as I could. I'm sure Lyle did too."

"Did he ever mention being threatened by anyone?" Tony asks.

"A few times. The truth is Chris was somewhat paranoid. Thought the world was out to get him. And . . . obviously someone was, did finally get him, but the whole world wasn't, was it?"

"Who do you think killed him?"

"I have no idea," she says, "but he was a very successful criminal defense attorney for many years. Bet he knew where a lot of bodies were buried. Might not be a bad place to start."

I think about how desperate Chris had become and I wonder if maybe he reached out to former clients for work or perhaps even to blackmail them. I had often wondered how Chris was living, what he was doing to pay his bills. He didn't work—unless you count his full-time position of stalking and harassing our family. Maybe extorting former clients was how he did it. And maybe it caught up to him.

As Audrey's recording comes to an end, I grab my phone again and tap the final recording—that of Chris's former legal partners, Philip Conrad and Brad Rowland.

Both men sound like what they are—slick, wary, manipulative, expensive lawyers.

"Look," Philip is saying, "we're defense attorneys. Even if we knew something we couldn't tell you. But we don't know for sure that Chris Taunton ever did anything illegal."

"And we don't want to know," Brad adds.

"And yet you fired him," Tony says.

"We didn't fire him," Philip says. "We weren't his bosses. We were partners. We expressed our . . . ah . . . discomfort with some of his . . . practices and behaviors and we . . ."

"Agreed to go our separate ways," Brad says.

"Exactly. Agreed to go our separate ways."

"The guy is dead," Darlene says. "Why try to protect him?"

"Defending people is what we do," Brad says.

"But we're trying to find out who killed him," she says. "If you care anything about him at all . . . wouldn't you want to help us do that?"

"See previous answer," Philip says. "We're defense attorneys. We fight the powers that be."

"We're not the powers that be," Darlene says. "We're the
small town cops trying to find out who killed your former
partner."

"Are there any previous clients who might have wanted
Chris dead?" Tony says.

They don't respond.

"More likely it'd be the family members of victims the scum
he defended killed and raped and stole from," Darlene says.

"Anybody blame him for getting off the murderer of one of
their family members?" Tony asks.

Neither attorney says anything.

"How about jealous husbands?" Darlene asks.

Still no response.

"You really have nothing else to say," she says.

"There is one thing," Philip says. "If you do charge someone
with Chris's murder, tell him to give me a call. Our firm would
love to represent him."

24

Waiting.
Much of criminal investigation is waiting.
Waiting for records requests.
Waiting for returned calls.
Waiting for evidence to be processed.
Waiting for autopsies to be performed.
Waiting for DNA results.
Waiting for toxicology results.
Waiting for subpoenas.

Of course we don't just wait. We work while waiting. We do what we can while waiting for what we can't. This is a kind of law enforcement equivalent of the Serenity Prayer and is necessary for survival.

When there were no fingerprint matches—either in the arrested or applicant searches—for the female victim we found buried in the swamp on the backside of the Dead Lakes Campgrounds, we immediately began working on a DNA profile for her and any possible DNA her assailant may have left behind—something that requires weeks of waiting. When those profiles come back, we will upload them into CODIS and hope for a match.

CODIS is the FBI's Combined DNA Index System, which stores DNA profiles which can be searched by analysts. Many crimes are solved this way. It just takes a while.

The lab is also running ballistics tests on the bullet recovered from the victim.

While all this is being done, we are uploading all the information we have about our victim into the Florida and national data bases FCIC / NCIC, and since she might be on the younger side of the estimated age range the ME gave us, I've included the National Center for Missing and Exploited Children.

When the DNA profile is back we will include it, but for now we're putting the best descriptions we can, including all scars, marks, and tattoos.

Because of skin slippage and the overall decomposition of the victim's face, including a picture is not possible, but we do have a forensics artist working on a rendering of her, which we will include when we have it.

All of this requires time. And waiting.

I've also submitted a request to see the cards on all missing females with TAT RT FT—Tattoos on their Right Foot. I'm waiting for it.

While I'm waiting, I'm working, beginning to contact tattoo artists in hopes of finding out who did the work for her and identifying her that way.

I'm also continuing to work on Chris's case—in the background, unofficially, Reggie feeding me information as she can.

In addition to all that, I'm working my other part-time job as a chaplain at Gulf Correctional Institution.

This afternoon I'm in my office in the chapel working my way through a list of inmates who have requested to see me.

Most of them want things I can't do anything about—to switch dorms, to go on furloughs, to make personal phone calls from my office, to use the chapel in some way that is unapproved.

But occasionally a man in need walks in with something I can help him with, and that's why I'm here.

I can listen. I can give counsel. I can comfort. I can recommend books and support groups and spiritual practices. I can provide a modicum of humanity and compassion in this inhumane and merciless place.

There is much about being a chaplain that is frustrating and futile, but so far I have been unable to give it up. It's still a big part of me, of my identity, of my mission, of my calling.

Over the course of a single afternoon, I have helped a young man with certain mind management techniques to deal with his obsessive thoughts, I've given a recovering addict some perspective on the twelve steps, I've comforted a man whose grandmother is dying.

But when I leave the prison this evening, it will be my last two sessions that I carry with me and remember the most.

"You the chaplain that's a cop, right?" Cecil Capps says.

He's a small, youngish man with a speech impediment and the scars from cleft palate surgery.

There are no secrets in prison—not for very long anyway—and every inmate at the institution knows I also work for the Gulf County Sheriff's Department.

I nod. "I'm a sheriff's investigator."

"You workin' the Chris Taunton case?"

I shake my head. "It's assigned to another investigator in our agency."

"'Cause you got a conflict of interest, sure, but you can put me in touch with who is, right?"

I shake my head again. "I can't put you in touch with anyone," I say. "Is there anything spiritual I can help you with?"

"Thing is, I know who killed him," he says. "I worked for the crooked bastard—did all kinds of shit for him. I guarantee I know who killed him and why he was killed 'cause I know what he's been involved in."

"Oh yeah, what's that?"

"I'm not saying a word until I get a deal," he says. "Want some time off my sentence. I can help with the case, but I got to get somethin' for it."

"I'll tell the investigators on his case what you've said, but they're not going to even bother talking with you if you don't offer some kind of proof that what you're saying is true."

"You tell them it all comes down to drugs and fraud and it involves millions of motives. Tell them it has to do with insurance claims after hurricanes and BP money payouts. I know what I'm talking about and I can help y'all catch his killer, but I ain't sayin' another word about it without a deal in place."

A moment after Cecil leaves, my door opens again and Tommy McMillan is standing there.

"Tommy?" I say in surprise.

"Hey, John," he says, and it's jarring not to be called Chaplain Jordan in this environment and context.

He walks in and I stand and walk around to greet him.

I extend my hand to shake his, but he grabs me and hugs me like I'm his long lost best friend instead of the man who sent him to prison.

"It's so good to see you," he says. "You have no idea."

"Have a seat," I say, indicating one of the chairs across from my desk, as I return to my seat.

Tommy looks very different from the last time I saw him. Skinny jeans, Italian half boots, and stylish hoodie have been replaced by a too-big blue inmate uniform and black brogans. His once longish rock and roll hair is now a bad buzzcut. And his once tanned face with carefully manicured stubble is now pale, puffy, and clean shaven.

Tommy and Michelle McMillan had once been the hippest, coolest youth ministers in Wewa. Now he's a convicted felon doing hard state time and she's a prison widow trying to keep the rest of the world from caving in on top of her.

"How are you?" I ask. "What're you doing here?"

"I'm okay. Better now that I'm close to home. Michelle's tried to drive down to see me in South Florida, but she hasn't been able to much."

"I had no idea when I'd ever see you again," I say, "but I figured when I did you might be hostile toward me."

"You kidding? This is all on me. All you did was catch me. And even then you treated me so right. I never got to thank you for all you did for me and my family, for all you've done. I've been working hard to forgive myself and to get in a better place —emotionally and spiritually. Been working through my grief and guilt, trying to heal, to recover."

"That's great, Tommy," I say. "That really is. I'm glad you're using your time so wisely."

"And now that I'm close enough to see my wife and family and friends on a regular basis and have you for my pastor . . . it's hard to imagine life being much better until I get out."

"I'm sorry," I say, "but I can't be your chaplain. We have a prior relationship, Anna and I help Michelle. The DOC doesn't allow that. I'm shocked they transferred you back here anyway. I'm sure there are several staff and officers here who you knew before."

"Yeah, that's the beauty of it, that's a good thing. Makes me actually feel like a human being again."

"I'm sure it does and I get it, but the department will never let you stay here."

"All I have to do is keep my head down and not call any attention to myself," he says.

"I'm required to notify the warden of our prior relationship. Anyone who knows you is supposed to. Once the department knows they will move you. I'm sorry."

"But, John, I've worked so hard to get here. Please don't ruin it for me. Please don't take me from my family and friends, my support system again. Please."

"I'm sorry."

"Think about Michelle. I thought you were committed to helping people. You know this is better all the way around—for everyone."

"I wish there was something I could do," I say.

"There is. Don't report it. Don't do this to me and my family."

"I'm sorry. I really am. But I have to. I wish I didn't. But I do."

"You don't. I know you don't. I won't cause you any problems. I promise. Please, please just don't take my family away from me again. Please. John, I'm begging you."

25

B y the time I get home, Michelle is waiting for me.
She and Anna are standing down by the lake in our
backyard, backlit by the August evening sunset.

The girls are playing on their swing set, a small Jack Russell
and beagle mix puppy named Tater yapping nearby.

I stop to see the girls first, getting bunches of hugs and
kisses for my trouble and being shown several tricks on the
swings and slide.

I'm again amazed at how kind and patient Johanna is with
Taylor.

"You're the best big sister in all the world," I whisper to her.

She beams and begins to mother Taylor all the more.

By the time I reach Anna and Michelle most of the sun is
behind the pine trees and cypresses bordering the far side of
the lake, the sky above it a brilliant dusky pink-orange that
seems to shimmer.

Michelle is crying.

"Hey, handsome," Anna says and kisses me as I walk up.

Before we can finish greeting each other, Michelle turns to
me and says, "Tommy called me this afternoon."

I nod. "Figured that's why you're here."

"Please tell me he misunderstood you," she says. "He's got to have, right? There's no way you could do this to us."

"I'm sorry," I say, "but I don't have a choice."

"Of course you do. You always have a choice. Always. Do you have any idea of the hell I've been living in?"

"Actually, we do," Anna says. "We've been right here with you the whole way."

"Y'all have been very supportive, you have, and I appreciate it, I do, but being supportive is not the same thing as going through it. Not even close."

"Wasn't saying it was," Anna says, "just that we know what you've been going through."

"I have no life. No friends. No future. Tommy's wasn't the only life that ended when he went to prison. Mine did too. Maybe more so. I've tried to go see him but it's such a long drive and I have no money and my car's in such bad shape. But I miss him so much and I've tried so hard to see him, to be a good wife, to keep our family from totally disintegrating. The only bright spot in all this time, the only thing that has given me the least little bit of hope I might actually survive is that he's back up here, that he's close enough for me to see. I honestly didn't think I was going to make it. And it wasn't easy. We fought very hard to and it took so long and so much, but . . . we finally got it done. And now you're wanting to undo it. It's like you're trying to take him away from me all over again."

"John didn't take him away from you the first time," Anna says.

Ignoring Anna, Michelle's glare bores into me. "Just don't do anything. That's all you have to do—nothing. How hard is that?"

"As soon as the department realizes they've sent him to the county where he committed his crime they'll move him anyway," I say. "It doesn't matter what I do, but I'm required to—"

"You always follow the rules, is that it, John? Always do what you're supposed to?"

I don't say anything. It's a ridiculous and rhetorical question, but it is something I think about often. Do I apply laws, rules, principles arbitrarily? Conveniently? When it suits my own purposes? I don't believe I do, and yet I can point to decisions I've made, actions I've taken that could support a case being made on either side. I had lost my first marriage over a principled decision in a challenging situation. It hadn't been easy but I had done it. It's a signpost of sorts, but there are others that contradict it.

"That what you're doing in the investigation into the death of her ex-husband?" Michelle asks.

"That's not fair," Anna says.

But it is. It's a very fair and relevant question. One I've been asking myself.

"Why even have a rule that an inmate can't be in a prison in the town he came from?" Michelle says. "Seems like cutting these men off from family and community, from any kind of love and civility is the worst thing you can do."

"I'm not saying it's not," I say. "But . . ."

"But what?"

She is upset and angry, our conversation charged with stress and negativity, and it's incongruous with the soft splendor of sunset, the serene stillness of the lake, and the shrieks and laughs and yelps of happy children playing with their jubilant, jumpy puppy.

"The policy, which I didn't create, is to avoid the conflicts of interests that lead to abuse and assaults and escapes. It's because of how many men in the past have used familiarity with family and friends to do them favors, because of the position it puts staff in. Prison is a perilous place. It puts all of us at risk if inmates know staff and officers and can get them to do things for them or use the information they have against them."

"You know Tommy and I won't ask you for any special favors," she says.

"What are you doing right now?" I ask.

"What?" she asks, and falters for a moment, before pulling it together. "You know what I mean. Nothing illegal. Nothing dangerous or—"

"Today Tommy hugged me and talked to me like a friend."

"You used to be his friend," she says.

"I still am. It's why I can't be his chaplain."

"You're gonna have him moved because he hugged you?"

"Moving him or not isn't up to me. That decision will be made by others. I have to make the department aware that I know Tommy, that we have a prior relationship, that I was instrumental in his arrest."

"But—"

"I will also tell them none of that will affect my ability to do my job, so they might let him stay, but I promise you this—I won't be the only staff member who lets them know. It's a small town. Tommy was popular, active in the community. Lots of people who work at the prison know him. I bet some of his former youth group members are now correctional officers. Most if not all of them will also report the prior relationship."

"You could talk to them," she says. "Y'all could do this one thing for us. This one little thing that could save our marriage, if not our actual lives."

"I'm happy to tell all this to the warden, to try to convince him to give Tommy a chance here. I will. And it may work. But what I can't do, what I won't, is try to cover up the fact that I and others know him and ignore safety protocols to do it."

"Well, thanks for nothing, John," she says. "Thanks for once again showing your true colors and only looking out for yourself."

She turns and storms off, but stops after a few feet and looking from the girls to us, adds, "I'm happy y'all have such a happy family and that y'all aren't burdened by the need to help others have what you have. That's got to make life simple and easy for you."

26

L ater that night I meet Merrill at the old gym on Main Street for what is supposed to be a pickup game, but he and I are the only ones to show up.

"What's the world comin' to, when you can't get young bucks to show up for a little pickup anymore?" he says.

"Doesn't mean we can't still lace 'em up," I say.

"No, it doesn't. Been a while since I schooled your old ass."

"And gonna be a while still."

The old gym, red brick on the outside, cinderblock on the inside, was once part of the old elementary school, but now stands alone since most of the school was torn down.

When we were kids, Merrill and I would play here after school with the kids from Wewa—sometimes as part of a structured Pottersville-versus-Wewa contest and sometimes in pickup games because we just showed up.

Some of the old-timers around town swear Wilt Chamberlin played in this gym, back when he was part of the Harlem Globetrotters, but I have no idea if it's history or legend.

As if suspended in time somehow, the gym looks and sounds and smells just the same.

The hardwood floor gleams, its thick polyurethane reflecting and refracting light in various directions. Ancient, wooden, half-height Wayne Rolling Gymstand bleachers run the length of the gym on either side, the wood worn and faded, the metal tags on them that say Wayne Iron Works almost illegible. Overhead the exposed giant wooden trusses hold high the white rafters and the now-antique metal heaters and hanging lights mounted to them.

The glass backboards are the same but at some point, still decades in the past, breakaway rims had been installed.

We start by stretching and shooting around to warm up.

Merrill and I had played basketball together for what seemed like our entire lives—street and backyard basketball, elementary, junior high, and high school, and now as grown, aging men the younger versions of ourselves wouldn't recognize.

Playing basketball, particularly with Merrill, had always been one of the most fun and rewarding physical activities I've ever done. I had stopped playing for a time when I first moved to Atlanta because of what happened to Martin Fisher, and thought I'd never play again, but eventually I returned to this game I so love, and think of Martin each time I step onto the court.

As we have aged, Merrill and I have both lost a step or two and lack the speed and endurance we once had, but because we had played consistently through the years, we play like men much younger than we are.

"What's happening with the case?" Merrill asks.

"Which one?"

"The motherfucker that tried to kill you and held your family hostage," he says, "*which one.*"

"Darlene and an FDLE agent named Tony Ford are plugging away at it," I say. "Reggie and I are keeping a close eye on it and running a little parallel investigation of our own."

"Sounds like somethin' you could use a PI on," he says. "When you gonna deal me in?"

"How about now? You can start by telling me about yours and Anna's movements that day."

"She took the kids to the park. I watched from the woods, keepin' an eye out for the bastard."

"Did he show?"

He nods. "He was in stealthy stalker mode, but nothin' get past ol' Eagle Eye Monroe."

"What'd he do?"

"Just hid and watched, never made a move toward them, just stared at 'em like he's in a trance or some shit."

"What did you do?"

"I watched too. Watched him watching them."

"You didn't confront him, give him a little tuneup, box his ears a bit?"

"I was in bodyguard mode. My job was to protect Anna, Taylor, and Johanna, not to be boxin' the ears of some—man, where do you come up with this shit? Boxing his ears."

It isn't lost on either of us that he avoided answering my question, that the response he gave me wasn't a denial of confronting, assaulting, or killing Chris. It was just a statement of his mission.

"That all I'm gonna get?" I ask.

He nods. "Sho enough is, so shoot for ball and let the spankin' begin."

"One thing before I do," I say. "If you're serious about helping . . . could you see if you can find a connection between Chris and a guy named Cecil Capps?"

"Sure. Who's he?"

I tell him.

He nods. "Consider it done."

Merrill

As John shoots for ball, Merrill thinks about what he should and should not tell him, and concludes he's told him enough already.

He's never known a better man, never had a better friend.

He knows there's nothing John won't do for him, that he will protect him at all costs—and that's exactly what Merrill is going to do for John.

He was at the park that day to protect John's family and that's what he did. That's what he's still doing.

Sometimes a man like John, with his nearly knight errant sense of morality and honor, with his commitment to being a particular kind of man, has to be protected from himself.

And that's precisely what he's doing—protecting John from himself and his impossible code. But . . .

He's left the door open a crack. He's let John know there is more to know, so if it comes down to it, if he absolutely needs to know, he'll know who to come back to.

I miss the 3 point attempt, so Merrill gets the ball first.

We're playing 2s and 3s to 21.

Merrill is both bigger and stronger than me. So I have a particularly difficult time defending him in the post. He can back me down pretty consistently. My best chance is to steal the ball before he starts his move, which is what I attempt to do during his first possession, but I miss and he makes an easy layup.

I take the ball up top, driving to the left, then stopping about halfway down the lane, spinning to the right, and pulling up for a midrange jumper, which goes in.

As usual, it's going to be a far more offensive than defensive game.

We continue this way for a while, both of us making and missing roughly the same amount, but I'm two ahead because I've made 2 3s.

As I dribble near the top of the key, the bouncing of the ball ricocheting its sound all over the hard surfaces of the gym, I say, "Did you see anyone else watching or even aware of Chris besides you and Anna that day?"

"Oh, you tryin' to distract me. Okay. Tell you what, you make this shot and I'll answer you. How 'bout that?"

He gets down lower, tightening his defense, determined not to let me score so he doesn't have to answer my question.

I act as though I'm going hard to the basket, but pull up for a fadeaway jumper on the right side of the lane. It's a close range, easy shot, and because I'm fading away, he is unable to block it.

Nothing but net.

"What was your question again?"

I smile. "Was anyone else watching or even aware of Chris at the park that day?"

"Pretty sure I saw your dad, Daniel and Sam, and Reggie and her mom ride through the park while we were there. Separately. And I can't be sure. There were probably others. A few times I could hear vehicles but couldn't see 'em 'cause of where I was. What's the score?"

"I'm up 18-14," I say and throw him the ball.

He quickly drives left, goes baseline, and shoots a reverse layup under the right side of the goal.

"18-16," he says.

"Yeah," I say, "game point."

He laughs. It's only game point if I make a 3, and not only am I shooting a very low percentage from 3 but he's going to be guarding up high to prevent me from making one.

I pump fake a 3 from the top, then drive in like I'm going to shoot a layup—something he's willing to let me do since it won't put the game away.

But instead of shooting a layup, I keep dribbling—under the basket, along the baseline, and into the corner, where I turn around and shoot a 3, which hits the back of the rim, bounces up, falls back in, rattles around a little, then drops through the net.

"Son of a bitch," he says.

"Good game," I say.

"We playin' best of 3 or 5?" he asks.

I laugh. "Thought that was it."

"Oh, hell no," he says. "I's just warming up."

27

"Took you a while to get to me," Randa says.

"Sorry."

"No need to be. You didn't bruise my ego or anything, I'm just surprised."

"I called to see if you were still in custody when I first heard Chris had been killed, if that makes you feel any better."

I'm interviewing Randa Raffield in the small interview room of the investigative division building. I could've driven up to the Liberty County jail and interviewed her there, but by doing it here, not only did I give her a chance to get outside, get some food, and be in a better setting, but I am able to record our conversation here—on both audio and video.

She nods. "That makes sense. Assuming they told you I was."

To the best of Patch McMyers' knowledge, Randa was in the holding cell of the Gulf County jail when Chris was murdered, but I'm not confident she was.

"Were you?" I ask.

Randa is brilliant and elusive. She vanished from the face of the earth and stayed that way for over twelve years—and could've stayed in limbo even longer if she had really wanted to. If anyone could escape from the county jail, kill Chris, and sneak back inside before anyone noticed, it would be her.

"In custody when Chris was killed?" she says. "That would be telling, wouldn't it? I'm not gonna do your job for you. Where's the fun in that?"

When I first met Randa she had blond hair and blue eyes and went by a different name. Today her hair is Auburn and her eyes are green—from all indications her natural colors. The only things about her appearance that haven't changed are the things that can't—her height and build and how pale her skin is. She's a smallish woman with an athletic, youthful bearing—at thirty-three she still has the body of the student swimmer she had been when she went missing at twenty-one.

"Of course, even if you were, doesn't mean you didn't have anything to do with it," I say. "You could've had it done."

Before being arrested, Randa had promised me she was going to kill Chris. In fact, that's what she was attempting to do when we apprehended her.

She nods. "In a variety of ways. I told you I would do it. You know I'm capable of it. So . . ."

She leans forward, withdraws the cardboard No Name coffee cup from the table between us, leans back and begins to sip on it again. I had offered to get her anything she wanted, but all she would let me get her was a cup of coffee from the No Name Cafe on Reid because she had heard one of the jailers talking about how good it is.

"Are you?" I ask.

"Capable?" she asks, lowering the cup away from her mouth. "You kidding? You've seen firsthand what I'm capable of."

"I know you held a guy hostage for an extended period of time," I say.

"A couple of guys," she says. "Don't forget Daniel. How is he doing by the way? He hasn't come to visit me yet. Why is that?"

"A couple of guys," I correct. "But I'm not sure you've ever killed anyone in anything but self-defense."

"That's sweet, John," she says. "It really is. I hope the jury will see it the same way you do—unless we reach a plea deal first."

"Am I wrong?" I ask.

"That if I've ever killed at all, I've only ever killed out of self-defense? I'll stipulate to that. Of course, people define it differently, that notion of self-defense."

"Did you kill Chris—out of self-defense or otherwise?" I ask.

"Did I tell you I would?"

I nod. "You did."

"Exactly," she says. "Still . . . figuring out or proving motive, means, and opportunity . . . that's gonna be tough. If I did do it . . . there's no way you could figure out how and prove it."

"You don't think so?"

"You've bested me a couple of times, John, I'll admit—you're the only man who ever has—but this is different."

"Is it?"

"Very."

"How?"

"The level of complexity involved, the precision it would require, a million other reasons."

"So you won't say whether you did it or had it done or not, but you are saying that if you did I'd never be able to figure out how, let alone prove it?"

"Is that what I said? Sounds a little verbose for me."

"Please," I say, "clarify in your own words."

"Let's say . . . for the sake of argument . . . let's say you did it —you or Anna or maybe even Merrill—any of you. If one of y'all did . . . I've got no problem with you blaming it on me. You can say I did it or had it done. I can win two cases as easily as one. Would take the heat off you and the others. And like I said, I'd get off so I don't mind."

"That's a very generous offer," I say. "Thank you."

"Not a problem."

"But," I say, "if I didn't do it . . . and I really want to find out who did, it would help me to know for sure that you didn't, so I won't waste time investigating you."

"I could never be a waste of time," she says. "You should know that by now."

"I didn't say you were—or ever could be."

"Tell you what," she says. "If you want me to, I'll solve it for you. You give me copies of the case files, a complete murder book, and I promise you I'll be able to tell you who did it. But of course that assumes two things."

"Oh yeah? What are those?"

"That you don't already know who did it," she says. "And that you actually want him or her caught."

28

On my way home, I stop by Chris's small, old, rented home on Second Street.

The poorly constructed house appears about to implode, its rotting, termite-infested boards about to crumple in on themselves.

The dilapidated rental property sits next to a few others, just down from the old city hall and fire department, a couple of rows of aluminum building storage sheds, and across the street from a coin laundromat inside what used to be a dentist's office.

I find Reggie inside with Jessica Young, our crime scene officer, a couple of deputies in crime scene coveralls assisting her, and Darlene Weatherly. Tony and Arnie have already gone home for the day.

"How'd your interview with Randa go?" Reggie asks.

I hand her and Darlene a CD recording of it. "Not great. I'll try her again in the near future. She's enjoying playing too much right now."

"I'm not so sure it's such a good idea for you to be interviewing her or anyone else connected to Chris's case," Darlene says.

"Why's that?" Reggie asks. "John has a rapport with her that no one else does."

"But I thought you were working the female victim case," she says.

"I am."

"Why don't you think it's a good idea?" Reggie asks again.

"Conflict of interest," she says. "Even if it's just a perception . . . it could ruin our case."

"This coming from you or Tony Ford?" Reggie asks.

"I'm saying it as a friend," she says. "I'm just trying to do my job and protect my case from anything that could compromise it. I'm not gonna throw Tony or anyone else under the bus—including John—but y'all need to know what everybody's thinking and most people are saying."

"Which is?"

"That our department is trying to cover something up—or at least be in a position to if it comes to that. Look, I'm just saying be careful. Be discreet. Be less involved if you can. That's all."

"Thank you," I say. "I understand and I will."

"I asked John to drop by here," Reggie says. "I thought we'd all be here and could have a little impromptu staff meeting of sorts, but Tony Ford is already on his way back to Tallahassee and Arnie had to take his wife to a doctor's appointment in Panama City this afternoon."

"Hey, like I said," Darlene says with her hands up, "I'm just trying to look out for our department and this case. That's all. Have no other agenda."

"What're y'all doing here?" I ask Jessica. "I thought the house had already been processed."

As I ask her I look around at the sad, crumbling little

shelter that surely must somehow be a metaphor for Chris's life.

Even with all of us in it, it still feels lonely, hollow, barren. Even with the crime scene lights set up it seems dreary, dim, bleak. Even with our attention focused on it, the forlorn diminutive dwelling still seems forgotten.

"It had," she says. "At least in terms of your typical cursory potential crime scene once over, but because of the residue of drugs and some of the cash the FDLE lab found in the car, we decided to take a closer look."

"We're opening up walls and shit," Reggie says.

"And look what we found," Jessica says, nodding toward the kitchen.

We all step over to it and look inside.

On sheets of plastic draped across the kitchen table stacks and stacks of cash are laid out in neat rows.

"Had nearly a million in cash hidden in his hallway walls," Jessica says.

Reggie shakes her head. "Sorry son of a bitch had a checking account and would routinely get hardship handouts from local churches and what little extra money his folks could spare to send him and he's sitting on a cool million in cash."

"Any drugs, weapons, or anything else?" I ask.

"Just cold hard cash," she says.

"So he's been up to who knows what since he's been in town," Reggie says.

"It's possible he brought it with him," I say. "Had it hidden, put away for a rainy day and grabbed it when he got out of jail and moved here. Maybe to do with what Cecil Capps mentioned."

She nods. "Could be."

"Either way, you know what the old proverb says," I add.

"What's that?"

"Money in the wall is a motive for murder," I say.

"You just made that up, but you're not wrong," she says. "I'd say we're looking at a million motives—each one of them leading away from John's family and our department."

"This make you think any differently about Cecil's offer?" I ask.

"The DA is drawing up an agreement that says we'll talk to the judge on his behalf if he gives us solid, credible information that leads to the arrest and conviction of Chris's killer. It comes with no guarantees so I doubt he'll go for it, but we'll soon find out."

"That's another situation where I think it's best if you don't talk to him," Darlene says to me.

"I'm not," I say. "He came into my office. Told me about wanting a deal. I brought it to y'all. I haven't spoken to him since. And don't plan to."

She nods her approval.

"So if there are no drugs in the house," I say to Jessica, "what's the deal with the drugs found in Chris's car?" Glancing at Darlene I add, "Asking for a friend."

"The car was pretty clean," Jessica says. "Mostly just residue, traces. He could've given someone a ride who had it on them. He could have been around it and transferred it to his vehicle. Hard to say, but . . . there's just not enough of it."

"If he was dealing or using or—"

"We'd expect to see more."

As we walk toward our vehicles, I ask Darlene if I can speak with her for a moment.

"Sure. What's up?"

"I appreciate what you said in there and the difficult position you're being put in. I'm sorry it's this way for your first case."

She shrugs. "Is what it is. I can deal."

"I just want you to know I'm not going to do anything to compromise your investigation and I would never do anything to embarrass you. You have my word."

"That means a lot to me," she says. "Really does. Meant a lot to me that you gave me a CD of your interview with Randa too."

"Trust takes time to earn," I say. "I'm sure in time you and I will trust each other and rely upon one another the way Reggie, Arnie, and I do now. Just takes some time and testing. We'll all get there."

She nods. "I believe we will. And in the meantime you count on me not to do anything to compromise or embarrass you either."

29

"Had a couple of interesting phone calls today," Anna says. "One from Chris's mother, the other from Carla."

"Oh yeah?"

We are in our kitchen cooking dinner together. Well, she's cooking. I'm helping. Through the case opening above the oven, we can see the girls playing on the floor in the living room while watching a kids' adventure movie that involves birds and dogs. Beyond them, through the french doors, Tater is running around the backyard on his chain while evening slowly expands toward dusk.

Anna is standing at the stove. I'm across from her at the sink, though my upper body is twisted toward her.

"Audrey, that's Chris's mom, who he always told me was dead, says Chris's dad, Lyle, plans to hire a PI and a PR firm, both in an effort to attack you and the department and accuse us of killing Chris and covering it up."

"Can he afford that?"

"There are always those who charge cut-rate prices to exploit your grief," she says. "Hell, some'll do it for the publicity alone, but she says he's going to use his savings and mortgage his house."

"Why'd she tell us?"

"She has nothing to do with it and believes it will only make their pain and grief worse. She really wants to meet her grand-daughter before she dies and thinks if Lyle can meet her too that he might—that it might help him heal some and maybe he won't try to destroy our lives and his own in the process."

I think about it.

"Whatta you think?" she says.

"I think it's your decision and I'll support you in it and help with it either way," I say. "What kind of sense did you get from her on the phone?"

"I felt like . . . like even if none of the rest of it worked I wanted her to meet her grandchild. I may be projecting . . . probably am . . . but I found myself relating to her. She seems too kind and . . . she was realistic about Chris. I just thought . . . maybe . . . if the mother of a monster can be a decent person maybe the ex-wife of one can too."

I drop the knife in the sink and step over to her. Pulling her away from the stove, I spin her around and hold her.

I start to say several things, but stop each time, deciding instead just to hold her.

"How could I have married such a . . . man?" she says. "How could I have stayed married to him? What's wrong with me?"

I don't say anything, just continue to hold her, as the girls play and the pots on the stove go without stirring.

"That wasn't rhetorical," she says. "I'd like to hear your thoughts on the subject."

"Sorry. No one is responsible for who they marry as a kid—and that's what you were. You were still in high school when you started dating him. And then . . . trying your best to make it work, to figure it out and not fail . . . is commendable. And of course trying even harder for your unborn child . . . Chris was a professional liar, maybe even a highly accomplished sociopath."

"Sometimes I have nightmares about Taylor growing up to be just like him," she says. "Like she won't be able to escape the curse of his DNA."

"She has your DNA, and his is no match. Plus she'll have a lifetime of nurture from you and more love from both of us and her big sister than she'll know what to do with."

She nods her head against my shoulder and sniffles a little. "There's no doubt about that."

"Look at them," I say.

She turns and follows my gaze to the two precious little girls playing so sweetly and contentedly together on the rug on the living room floor.

"You're right," she says. "I'm being silly. And now I've burned dinner."

"Actually, that was my fault," I say. "I'll go pick us up something. What sounds good? You go in there with them and you'll have your faith in humanity restored by the time I get back."

"You've already done that," she says. "It's something you've done every single day I've known you."

After we place our order, I ask her what Carla said.

"She was just checking in. Wondered if we had made a decision yet. I think she's just nervous. We've got to make a decision soon, but in the meantime could you give her a call and reassure her? I tried to, but I'm sure hearing from you will do her the most good."

On my way to pick up dinner from the Tiki Grill, I call Reggie.

"I tried to talk to you at Chris's earlier this evening," I say, "but someone was always around."

"What's up?"

"I spoke to a witness who saw you and your mom at the Dead Lakes Campground the night Chris was killed."

"How credible?"

"Very."

"Well, we weren't exactly hiding," she says. "Pretty sure I even waved at Anna as we passed by."

"She's not the witness, by the way," I say. "She's saying very little about any of it."

"Wouldn't matter if she were. I'm assuming since you haven't already, you don't plan on telling me who the witness is."

"No reason to," I say. "He's a friend—of both of ours."

"What do you plan on doing with his statement?"

"Just what I'm doing," I say. "Sharing it with you."

"Does the witness plan on doing anything else with it?" she asks.

"No. Hell, I barely got him to tell me."

"Okay. Thanks. And for the record—yours if no one else's— I was just driving Mom around. We do that some . . . just to get her out of the house. Drove all over that evening. Just rode around and talked. Didn't get out of the car."

Reggie and Sylvia

"Who was that?" Sylvia asks when Reggie ends the call.

"John."

"I take it someone told him we were in the park that evening?"

"Uh huh."

"Will it be a problem?" Sylvia asks.

"Shouldn't be," Reggie says.

"Really? Why's that?"

"Witness only saw us the first time," she says. "When we wanted to be seen."

Driving home from Tiki Grill with our food, I call Carla.
"You okay?" I ask.

"Yeah, just stressin'. Ready to have this settled."

"We'd like to meet again and talk some more about it," I say. "And we thought if you're willing for us to, we might go to your next doctor's appointment with you."

"Sure, I'd love that."

"One of the things I want you to think about," I say, "is if you're sure you really don't want to raise your baby yourself. Because if you do, we would help in every way imaginable— support, money, babysitting, anything you need. That way you'd get everything we can offer, but you'd still get to raise your child."

"That's unbelievably generous of you," she says, "and I'll think about it some more, but I have been thinking about it, have been looking at it from every imaginable angle and I always reach the same conclusion . . . I'm just not ready. Now is not the time for me."

"And what happens when in a few short years it is the time for you?" I say.

"I won't come asking for your baby—and that's what it'll be, *your* baby—I'll have my own when it's my time. You have my word on that. You don't have to worry about growing attached to your son and having me try to take him from you. It won't happen."

"Think about everything from every possible angle all over again," I say, "and we'll get together soon and talk about all of it."

30

A couple of nights later, after Anna and Taylor and most of the country have gone to bed, and I've called and said goodnight to Johanna who is back with her mom for the new school year, Merrill and I drive to Panama City.

It's a dark night, and quiet, the rural roads and city streets mostly empty.

We're heading to an area on 15th Street where Panama City begins to transition into Panama City Beach, where bars, strip clubs, and tattoo parlors are concentrated in a few city blocks.

I had bribed Merrill out of bed with his fiancé, Zaire, with the promise we could stop by Joe's Corner Pub on the way back for wings, but as we near the Gold Nugget strip club, he seems to have other things on his mind.

"Sure they's nobody in there we need to interview?"

"You tell me," I say. "I'm sure there is, between all the cases you're working."

"Speaking of," he says. "I think Cecil Capps may be legit. Chris was his attorney and business partner in some pretty shady shit back in the day. Don't know how up-to-date his info is, but . . . he knew some shit at some point."

"DA's gonna offer him a deal to talk," I say.

"Fucked up system," he says. "The more shit you do, the more shit you know, the more you have to trade, the more chances you skate."

I nod.

"Cecil was involved in all kinds of fraud," he says. "Probably means Chris was too. Maybe where a lot of his ill-gotten gain came from. Insurance fraud. Bank fraud. Even got caught filing fraudulent BP claims."

Following the Deep Horizon oil spill, BP has been paying billions of dollars in damages and fines to Gulf Coast governments and businesses—a process that attracts the fraudulent like flies.

"Worth looking into even deeper," I say.

"I noticed as I was looking over his clientele that Chris represented a lot of alleged drug dealers too. That's an easy population to skim from—either by milking billable hours or misappropriating retainers, things he had been accused of before. Could've been taken out as part of some *payback's a bitch* kind a shit."

"Maybe we'll be able to trace the money we found in his house."

"Be better for all us we can find some cartel to pin it on."

We reach Midnight Ink and turn in.

Midnight Ink is in an old building that was probably at one time a convenience store. It's located between a biker bar and a squalid extended stay motel. Across the street are a strip club and an all-night diner that specializes in pills.

Suddenly, we're surrounded by colorful fluorescent highlights. Hanging in the windows and flickering on the signs by the road. Beer and liquor logos. The flamingo pink of Florida Lotto. Gas prices. Vacancy.

We get out in the dark neon night and walk in, the incessant electric hums and buzzes of tattoo guns filling our ears the moment we open the door.

The bright, loud joint is somehow both cluttered and open.

Beyond a seating area comprised of a couple of old mismatched pleather couches where two scantily clad teen girls sit with their feet under them playing on their phones, three tattoo artists are hunched over clients stretched out in chairs along the back wall.

In disconcerting contrast to the look and feel and vibe of both the place and the people in it, the music playing in the background sounds like a cheaply produced Enya knockoff.

No one in the entire establishment even looks up at us except for Bobby Ink, the artist in the middle chair and the man we've come to see.

"Is that motherfuckin' John Jordan creepin' my candy store in the middle of the night?" Bobby Ink says. "Is it?"

"Bobby," I say.

Bobby Ink is a smallish, narrow-framed man with what looks like just a little more Native-American than African-American in him. He has long, fine, straight, silky black hair and a wide, dark, hairless face with deep set black eyes.

"Must be some serious shit you come to see Bobby about, you brought that hard nigga right there with you now."

"Just got a few questions for you," I say. "You got a minute?"

"For you, I got all the time in the world. Can we talk while I work? I got a baby in desperate need of some new shoes."

"Not a problem," I say.

"Then step into my office."

We walk around the seating area, past the half-wall, and into the well-lit studio space in the back.

"Merrill," Bobby says.

"Bobby," Merrill replies.

"You Chatty Cathies through?" I say.

A woman without a top on is lying face down on the chair,

her large, pale breasts pressed against the chair and spilling out on either side of her. Bobby Ink is filling in some of the rotting flesh hanging from a zombie Rottweiler in a photorealistic post-apocalyptic scene from a makeup counter in a dead-infested department store in an abandoned mall.

"Proceed," Bobby says.

"I'm trying to identify a homicide victim and all I have is a picture of her tattoo," I say. "I have no idea if she's from this area or had the work done here, but I'm starting with you."

"Always start with the best when you can," he says.

"How many shops are there in town?" I ask. "Would you recognize most of the local artists' work?"

He shakes his head. "We've got about ten shops in town and another fifteen or so on the beach. And not only is there a big turnover, but we have guest artists come into town all the time —especially during spring break and Thunder Beach. Not to mention a lot of the guys around here are all doing the same damn thing—some version of new school Americana shit. Big, bold lines, bright colors. A real 40s and 50s feel. Unless what you have is real distinctive or includes the guy's signature . . . Like me, I do photorealistic work. Some guys do fine line and extreme detail work, but otherwise . . . What's the image of? Anything exotic or unusual?"

"'Fraid not," I say. "It's a baby's footprint with the name Brandon written across the top of it. All of it in black."

"Oh shit."

"I know."

"I'm sure I can't help, but let me take a look at it just to be sure," he says.

He puts his gun down and I hand him the picture.

He shakes his head. "You're gonna have to do store by store. And there's no guarantee it was even done in the area, right? Nice thing is . . . if it was . . . the artist will have a copy of the client's ID and a detailed description of the art, and most of these places are open well into the night. You can probably hit up ten tonight if you really hustle."

"Ain't y'all got some sort of network or some shit?" Merrill says. "You upload the picture and we go have a beer at the Nugget while you wait to hear back from the guys . . . and girls."

"Most tattoo artists I know are anarchists," he says. "Even if there was a group . . . I don't know anyone who would join it. I'm tellin' you man . . . finding the guy—"

"Or girl," the woman face down in the chair says in a muffled voice.

"Or woman," Bobby corrected, "that's the part that's gonna be a bitch."

"Or bastard," Merrill says.

31

The next morning, after sleeping in a little, I'm in the shower when the call comes.

"Where are you?" Darlene asks.

"Still at home. Why?"

"Good. Tony wants us to interview Anna first thing this morning—plans on surprising her, counting on you being at work."

"Thank you, Darlene. I really appreciate you letting me know."

"Not cool to be so underhanded with the wife of one of our own," she says. "I know he's under a lot of pressure and all . . . but still."

"What kind of pressure?" I ask.

"The victim's dad, Lyle Taunton, calls him and his superior every single day, and started talking to the media a couple of days ago. He's been on all the TV news stations, and there was a big story in the *Tallahassee Democrat* this morning, claiming corruption and cover-up, that we're all conspiring together to help you get away with murder. He's feeling the heat, but it doesn't justify ambushing Anna like this."

"Does if he thinks she did it."

By the time Tony and Darlene arrive, Anna and I are ready and waiting for them—though what it appears like we're doing is just having breakfast together. Our sitter has Taylor at the park—something that hasn't happened since Chris was released from jail and began stalking us.

W hen the doorbell rings, I answer it.

"John?" Tony says, his voice rising with his eyebrows. "I'm, ahem, glad you're here. We tried to get here before you went to work."

"All you had to do was let me know you were coming and I could've rearranged my schedule, but anyway I'm here. Had a late night of looking for the female victim's tattoo artist, so I'm moving sort of slow this morning. What's up?"

"Now be a good time to talk to Anna about her statement?" he says.

"I'm sure it will be," I say. "Come in, and I'll ask her."

They step into the mudroom and wait there while I step back into the eating area at the far end of the galley kitchen and talk to Anna.

"N ow's great," I say. "Y'all come on in here. Want some coffee or juice or anything?"

"We're good," he says.

"I'll take some OJ if you have some," Darlene says.

"Coming up. Y'all have a seat at the table. Okay to just do it here?"

"Sure," Tony says. "Anywhere is fine. This is just a formality. Us checking boxes, being thorough."

I return with Darlene's juice and sit next to Anna and directly across from Tony and Darlene.

"Mind if I record our conversation?" Tony asks Anna.

"Actually, I'd prefer it," she says, adding as she swipes and presses apps on her phone until it's recording. "In fact, I'll record it too. For a backup."

"Great idea," he says, and it sounds like everything else he has said since he has been here—hollow and insincere. "Okay, this is just a follow-up to the written statement you already gave. Like I said we're trying to win the thorough award."

Anna nods.

"Rather than us rehashing everything from your statement," he says, "would you mind just taking us through your afternoon and evening again?"

His asking her to do it this way has nothing to do with him not wanting to rehash her written statement and everything to do with him wanting a separate, verbal account so he can compare it for inconsistencies."

"Sure," she says. "No problem."

"John was in Atlanta. I had both girls by myself. We got up and had breakfast and—"

"You can skip ahead to the late afternoon-evening of that day," he says.

"When I took the girls to the park to play?" she asks.

She is calm and composed, appearing like a cooperative witness with nothing to hide.

"Great," he says. "Yes. Why'd you do that?"

"We were all getting a little stir crazy, wanted to get out of the house."

"Sure," he says, "but why the Dead Lakes Campground? Why not Lake Alice Park? It's a much better playground and is just like a quarter mile from your house. You could've walked it."

"The girls prefer the park at the campground. Plus it kills more time. John wasn't going to be home anytime soon, so . . ."

"And you weren't scared of Chris?" he asks.

"Scared of Chris?" she asks.

"That he would harass you or try to bother you in some way?"

"With him, that was always a possibility, but we didn't let it stop us from going on with our lives. We couldn't, or he had won."

"Did you have someone helping you? Guarding you?"

"It was just the girls and me," she says. "I knew a deputy drove through the campgrounds a few times each evening and I could call someone if I needed help. But I didn't think I would need any. Like most stalkers and harassers, Chris was a weak little man who would crumble if you confronted him."

"And did you?"

"What?"

"Confront him?"

"When?"

"Anytime that day?"

"No, I didn't."

"But you did speak to him, didn't you? A few times, in fact." He opens a folder sitting next to him on the table and pulls out a copy of Chris's phone logs. "He called you several times that day, and you even called him."

"Did he? Did I?"

"That's what the phone logs say," he says.

"Well, then it must have happened," she says. "Phone logs don't lie, do they? Just ask Adnan Syed."

Darlene, content to let Tony do all the talking, has yet to utter a single syllable. Head down, taking notes, she rarely even lifts her head or looks up.

"Do you not remember calling him or him calling you?"

"Over the course of these months and months of harassment, I have blocked his number, but each time I do, he gets a new phone or borrows one or uses a service to display a different number.

Most of the time when a new number pops up I don't answer it, I wait to see if the caller leaves a voicemail, but that day . . . with John in Atlanta and Susan with her new boyfriend whose number I don't have, I may have answered or even called the number back."

"May have? You don't remember?"

"I remember Chris calling at some point," she says. "I remember calling back a number I didn't recognize and it being him, sure. I just don't remember if it was Friday or Saturday or Sunday."

"According to the log it was Sunday, the day he was killed," Tony says.

"Then it must have been."

"What did y'all talk about?"

"The usual stuff—*Why are you doing this? Please stop. This isn't doing anyone any good—especially your daughter.* Stuff like that. I always tried to reason with him, to appeal to the better man I used to know and to the father inside him. It never worked, but I never completely gave up on getting through to him either."

"Did it get heated? Were there threats?" Tony asked.

She shakes her head. "As odd and off and futile as the notion was . . . Chris's conversations with me were always him trying to woo me, trying to convince me he was a good guy, that he had been misunderstood and falsely accused, and just wanted us to be a family again. It was surreal, but it was never angry or threatening."

Much of what Anna is saying is, at best, only partially true, but she's convincing. Scarily convincing. I know the relative truth or falsehood of most of her statements, and she's still convincing me.

"When you called him that evening," Tony says, "why'd it last so long? It was a fourteen-minute phone call."

"For the reasons I mentioned earlier. I was trying to reason with him, encouraging him to let go, to start seeing a counselor, that sort of thing."

"And that was it?"

She nods. "Pretty much. More or less."

"Okay," he says, and he is unable to conceal his frustration. "When you came home from letting your daughters play at the campground, did you leave your house again?"

She nods.

"Where did you go?"

"I realized I needed a few additional ingredients to make dinner so I went to get them and once we got home, Johanna realized she left her little headphones at the playground so I went back to see if I could find them."

"Did you?"

"I did."

"Did you go alone or take the girls with you?" he asks.

This question makes me think he knows or has heard something and is asking for a very specific reason.

"I left them here with the teenage girl from next door who babysits for us sometimes."

"Did you see anyone while you were there? Anything suspicious?"

"No, but I was only there a few moments. It was dark by then. I left my car running, the lights pointed toward the playground, got out, looked around for the headphones until I found them, got back in and left."

"And you didn't see Chris?'

"No."

"Or anyone else?"

"Sorry, I didn't."

"How close did you get to the first pavilion where Chris's body was found?"

"Very, and I can tell you at that time his body wasn't there. Nothing was in the pavilion."

"That was pretty late," Tony says. "Do you always feed your daughters dinner so late?"

She shakes her head. "No. I usually have them on a better schedule than that. We were just all out of whack that day, out of our normal routine."

"Yes you were, and I can't help but wonder why."

32

Though completely composed while Tony interviewed her, the moment he and Darlene left, Anna broke down and began to cry.

I held her without saying anything for a long moment.

"I'm okay," she says. "Just nerves. Just needed to cry my stress out."

"Let it all out," I say. "Take your time."

"I wish you didn't have to go to work today," she says.

"I don't. I'll call Reggie and tell her—"

"Tell her . . . Tell her you'll still be working, just here with Taylor and me. Oooh, I've got an idea. Why don't we go to Tallahassee for lunch? We could go by and introduce Taylor to her grandmother and see if she's still willing to help with Lyle."

I miss Johanna all the time when she's not here with us, and it particularly pierces my heart when we're talking about doing something as a family in her absence.

I nod. "Sounds good. We should see if Carla wants to go with us. Give us a chance to talk to her some more."

"Oh, that's a great idea," she says. "I'll call her while you call Reggie."

T wo hours later, we're knocking on Audrey Taunton's door at St. John of the Cross Assisted Living Community.

"Come in," a soft, elderly voice says.

When we open the door, Audrey, who is sitting in a recliner in her pajamas in the small, warm room, looks confused—until she sees Taylor. Then she bursts into tears.

"Oh, you brought her to see me. Oh, thank you. Thank you. Thank you."

The moment I saw Lyle Taunton at the crime scene I knew who he was because he looked like an older version of his son, but I can see no trace of Chris in his mom.

Audrey Taunton is stout in the way some older women are, shaped like a bell—smaller on the top and big-bottomed. She has curly gray hair longer than most women her age wear it, pale, wrinkled skin, and small blue eyes that seem to swim around in sockets that are too big for them.

She pushes herself up slowly, stands for a moment, then starts walking toward us. "I'm fine once I get going. Just takes me a minute. Two new knees. Come in. Come in. Thank y'all so much for coming to see me."

What St. John of the Cross Assisted Living Community calls an "apartment" is actually about the size of a large hotel room. Besides a small bathroom, Audrey's entire living area is a single room with a double bed, a seating area, and a small kitchenette.

"I'm your grandmother," Audrey says to Taylor. Then to Anna, "Can I hold her? I'm steadier than I look. Just takes me a minute to get going."

"This is Grandma Audrey," Anna says to Taylor. "Can you say *hey* like a big girl?"

Though acting shy, Taylor says, "Hey Grandma Audrey."

"I'm John, and this is our friend, Carla," I say.

"Nice to meet you both," she says. "Y'all come in and have a seat. Would you like some tea or coffee or anything?"

"We're good," I say. "Thank you."

Anna says, "I'm sure she'll go to you in a little while. Let's just give her a little while to get comfortable here."

"Of course. Sit down. Please."

We join her in the seating area, and at first, there's an awkward moment of silence.

"I can't believe he kept us apart for all these years," Audrey says. "I'm so sorry for . . . Well, for everything he did. That's not the way I raised him, I assure you of that."

"In the end," Anna says, "we're all responsible for our own actions."

"I saw Dylan Klebold's mother interviewed a few years back," Audrey says, "he was one of the young men who killed his classmates at Columbine, and I remember thinking—this was before I knew about any of the stuff Chris had done—I remember thinking *how can she live with herself?* What enormous pain she must be in. And she has to bear it all alone. And now . . . I know at least some of what she feels. And of course, now there are school shootings all the time. What in the world's going on? I don't even recognize this country anymore. And all the parents of all those killers can't be monsters. They just can't all be. I'm not a monster. Anyway . . . I'm truly sorry for everything Chris did or tried to do to you and your family."

Anna blinks back tears and says, "Thank you. That means more than you'll ever know."

I had been skeptical about us coming to see Audrey, but witnessing the healing taking place in Anna lets me know just how wrong I was to be.

"I don't blame you for divorcing him or anything that happened," Audrey says. "I just ask that you don't blame me . . . for who he became . . . for what he did."

"Thank you. I don't."

Audrey turns to Carla. "So young lady, what's your story? I take it you're with child."

"I am," Carla says, and candidly begins to tell Audrey all about herself and her situation.

"My my, what a smart and forthright young woman you are," Audrey says. "It's very refreshing. Your baby is lucky to have you for a mother—no matter your circumstance."

"Thank you."

"Children will break your heart," she says. "Love them and let them."

Carla nods but doesn't say anything.

There's a moment of awkward silence.

Anna starts to say something, but Audrey speaks first.

"Carla?" she says, "Could you do me a favor?"

"Sure."

"Could you go look in the console of my car and get the two plastic bags in it? The keys are in that bowl on the table by the door, and it's parked in spot seventeen."

As soon as Carla is gone, Audrey leans forward and says, "Y'all didn't bring her because she's carrying Chris's baby or anything like that, did you?"

"No," Anna says, shaking her head. "Nothing like that."

"It's funny in the moments when I thought she might be carrying his child, another grandchild . . . I began to think about what I might do to help her. The poor dear seems like she could use a bit of help. Anyway, I thought to myself if you were willing to help her some if she were carrying your grandchild you should help her though she isn't. Do some good in the world to make up for some of the bad. I plan to leave everything I have, which isn't much, but . . . to Taylor, but I was thinking . . . maybe I can help Carla a little now and again and leave her a little too."

"That's a lovely idea," Anna says. "Really kind of you."

"I really shouldn't be driving anymore, but I haven't quite gotten used to the idea of giving it up yet. After my knees are completely healed, I'll see if I can, but if I can't . . . If I'm forced to part with it . . . maybe I could give Carla and the baby my car."

"That's so sweet of you," Anna says. "Maybe it won't come to that—I hope you'll still be able to drive—but if it does . . . I'm sure she could really use it."

"Can't tell you how many operations I've had over the past few years—back and arm and knee. If I'm not in too much pain to drive, then I'm on too much pain medication to drive. If it stays that way . . . Anyway, we'll see. And as much as I'd love to save it for Taylor, it won't be worth having by then. Plus they'll probably have flying cars by then anyway."

When Carla returns, she places the keys back in the bowl and hands Audrey the bags.

With arthritic-misshapen fingers, Audrey reaches into the first bag and brings out a piece of hard candy. "Look what Grandma Audrey has for you," she says to Taylor. "Would you like a butterscotch?"

Taylor looks at Anna. Anna nods.

Taylor walks over to Audrey.

"Here you go," Audrey says, holding out the piece of candy. "Think I could have a hug in exchange for it?"

Taylor leans in, and Audrey hugs her for a long moment, then opens the candy for her. As she does, she looks at Carla. "What'd you think of my little car?"

"It's nice."

"I was telling Anna and John I may have to get rid of it soon. May not be able to drive anymore. I'll know in a few weeks after my next doctor's appointment. If I have to give it up . . . I'd like to give it to you."

"*What*?"

"If I can't have it . . . I want you to. You and the baby. I really don't need to be driving anymore anyway. I just don't like the idea of not being able to. Anyway, it's a good little car, and when I do have to give it up, I want you to have it."

"Really? I mean . . . Are you sure?"

"Really. I'm positive. I can't undo what Chris has done, but . . . I can do my little part to help make the world a little better place. The way John and Anna do."

As if realizing somehow that Grandma Audrey is doing something nice for Carla, who she has come to adore, Taylor remains leaning against her even after she releases her from the hug.

From the other plastic bag, Audrey removes a pen and a checkbook and starts scribbling on the top check. "What's your last name, Carla?"

"Pearson. Why?"

"'Cause I want to give you a little something for the baby and yourself. Make sure you're eating right and getting plenty of sleep. Take care of yourself, and you're taking care of the baby. This isn't much, but use it on yourself for whatever you need. And when you do just tell yourself this is from Grandma Audrey."

"Oh my God, thank you so much, Grandma Audrey," Carla says and moves over to hug her.

Taylor gets wrapped up in the hug between Carla and Audrey and likes it.

I glance at Anna to see if her eyes reveal any sadness at the possibility that Carla might keep the baby, but she shows none.

"That is so generous of you," Anna says to Audrey. "Thank you."

"It's more than my own grandmother has ever done for me," Carla says. "A lot more. But . . . you should know . . . I plan to put my baby up for adoption . . . So. . . I understand if you'd rather give the car and money to someone else."

"Of course not," she says. "It's yours. And I'm sure you'll make the best decision you can about your baby and everything else, and I hope this little bit I'm doing helps you no matter what you do."

The door to Audrey's room swings open and Lyle Taunton is standing there.

I stand and face him.

"Just what the fuck is going on in here?" he says.

"None of your business, Lyle," Audrey says. "Got nothing to do with you."

"These people killed your son," he says, his eyes locking onto mine. "Or don't you care?"

Though standing like he's ready for a fight and holding a tire iron in his right hand, he makes no move to come any farther into the room.

"Quit acting like a jerk and come meet your grandchild, Lyle," Audrey says.

"My attorney filed a wrongful death suit against you two this morning," he says. "You . . . fucks . . . aren't going to get away with killing my boy. And I'm petitioning the court for custody of Chris's child. I'll meet her when she's mine."

He then turns and walks away.

33

"I still can't believe she gave me two hundred dollars and may give me her car one day," Carla is saying.

We are sitting at Ted's Montana Grill off of Appalachia Parkway having a late lunch.

Co-founded by Ted Turner, the media magnate behind such cable networks as TBS, TNT, and CNN, Ted's Montana Grill is my favorite place to eat in Tallahassee and we come here nearly every time we're in town.

I always get the same thing—the bison meatloaf sandwich on ciabatta with salt and pepper onion rings. Carla and Anna are both picking at farmhouse salads, and Taylor is putting a serious hurting on a grilled cheese and french fries.

"I'm so glad she did," Anna says.

"It's just so overwhelming," Carla says. "I feel guilty . . . Like I shouldn't take it."

"You most certainly should," I say. "You have to. It's too great a gift, too much of an opportunity for you not to."

"Can't believe what an asshole her ex-husband is," she says.

"It's grief," Anna says. "He's not normally like that."

"He probably genuinely believes we killed his son," I say.

"Maybe," Anna says, "but I bet more than anything else he feels guilty. Wasn't much of a dad to Chris when he was growing up."

"He won't be able to take Taylor away from you, will he?"

Anna and I both shake our head emphatically. "No," Anna says. "He won't."

"Good."

"John said he talked to you about us helping you—financially and in every other way—if you keep the baby," Anna says.

Carla nods.

"Given that . . . and now knowing Audrey plans to give you some money each month and maybe even the car one day . . ." Anna says. "Have you thought any more about keeping it?"

She nods again. "I have. I feel like I've thought about every possible scenario about a billion times."

"That's good," Anna says. "It's too important a decision not to."

"And I just . . . If I had all the money in the world, I'd still think the best decision for me, and the baby, is to put him up for adoption. I just know I'm not ready. I just know for certain this is the very best thing I can do for him."

"*Him*?" Anna asks.

"Yes, the ultrasound showed a little winkie," she says. "Well, not little. It's the right size. I'm saying it's—that everything is little."

"A boy," Anna says. "You're having a boy."

"I'm going to put my baby up for adoption," she says. "I'm not going to change my mind. It would be a dream come true for you two to adopt him, but . . . If you can't . . . I'll understand. I just want you to know I'm not going to regret this later and change my mind. And even if you decide not to adopt him, I'm still going to do it, so . . ."

"Okay," Anna says. "Thank you for . . . Thanks for letting us know. Can you give us a little while longer to talk about it and make a final decision? I promise we won't keep you waiting long."

"Of course. I get it. You already have two. It's a big commitment. I just . . . Well, I hope you will. You two are the very best gift I could ever give my baby."

Our conversation wanes as we each begin to finish our meals in earnest.

In the intervening silence, my thoughts return to my current cases, and, as I do in all spare moments like these, I let my mind wander over the details, trying to examine the various pieces from different angles, asking myself and the evidence any and all questions that occur.

I think about the brutality with which Chris was beaten, the coldness with which the female victim was executed, and the differences between the two. I think about the blood trail and the way the killer prolonged Chris's death and the shallow grave the young woman was buried in. I think about the money in Chris's house and the likely illegal activities he had been involved in for many years, and how the way in which he was killed didn't seem like it had anything to do with money or business—illegal or otherwise, and I wondered if that was intentional? Was the excessive violence a form of staging—as much as sitting his body at the picnic table with a hood over his head and knife in his chest?

Taylor finishes first and begins to draw and color on the paper tablecloth—the activity that most likely inspired her to eat as quickly as she did.

As the rest of us wrapped up, Carla excused herself and went to the restroom.

"I know we need to have a long conversation later," Anna says, "probably several of them, but . . . can you tell me how you're leaning right now?"

"I don't need to talk any more about it unless you do," I say. "I think we should do it."

She actually lets out a squeal, covers her mouth, then knocks an empty glass over as she lunges forward to hug me.

"Me too," she says. "Oh, John, I'm so excited. This makes me so happy. So, so happy. Are you absolutely sure?"

"I am. Are you?"

"Beyond certain."

When Carla returns, Anna jumps up and says, "Yes. Our answer is yes. If you're sure."

"Are y'all sure?" Carla asks.

"Are you sure?" Anna says.

"I'm—" Carla begins, then bursts into tears.

At first, I think they are tears of joy, but as she sinks down to her seat, I can tell she is upset.

"What is it?" Anna asks as she drifts back down into her own seat.

"Are you okay?" I ask.

"Have you changed your mind?" Anna asks. "It's okay if you have. We'll help you give your baby the best life possible."

"I . . . I just . . . I feel so guilty," she says.

"About?" Anna asks.

"Y'all are being so good to me—John always has. And now Grandma Audrey who's not even my grandma and I . . . I'm just . . . I haven't been honest with y'all."

"About what?" Anna says.

"I'm seeing this guy stationed at Tyndall Air Force Base," she says. "Best guy by far I've ever been involved with. He's older and mature, settled and he's really, really good to me."

"Okay?" Anna says.

"He's TDY at Thule in Greenland right now," she says. "He's already said he wants to marry me when he gets back. And I want to. God, I want to marry him and be taken care of and happy for once in my life, but . . . I . . . We had an argument.

Wasn't even a bad one. But I panicked and in a moment of weakness I . . . I slept with an old boyfriend, and I got pregnant. My fiancé doesn't know I'm pregnant and . . . I can actually have the baby and give him up for adoption before he gets back and he'll never know. But I feel . . . I've felt so bad not being completely honest with you guys. And the truth is . . . Well, John's opinion of me means more than about anyone's, and I just couldn't bear to tell you the truth, but then I just couldn't keep it from you anymore. No matter what you think of me I have to be honest, have to come clean."

34

"What are you really doing here?" I ask.

I'm back at the Dead Lakes Campground talking to Captain Jack Patterson. We're standing down by the pond in early evening, the bubbling, gurgling, and splashing sounds of the fountain a soothing soundtrack for our conversation.

"Well it ain't looking for Bigfoot, I can tell you that," he says.

"Then why?"

"Do you know how many people go missing or are murdered in places like this each year?"

"No."

"Neither does anyone else because no one is keeping up with them," he says. "But it's astronomical. The problem is . . . It involves so many different jurisdictions, agencies, counties, states, and the fuckin' federal government. It's an epidemic, and I'm working to expose it."

It had rained earlier and cooled off everything a bit. The evening is pleasant, the park filled with people out for an evening stroll, walking their dogs, or going for a golf cart ride.

As if taking her neighborhood watch duties a little too seriously, Evelyn Hillman looks like she's actually on patrol.

HC and Georgia Thompson are out walking with what looks to be their children, grandchild, and great-grandchild. The middle-aged couple with them, presumably their kids, appear to have rebelled against their hippie parents. They couldn't look more conservative upper-middle-class Southerner if they ordered a kit from Banana Republic. Their daughter, who's dressed nothing like them, looks sad and it appears her mother is bogarting time with her baby.

"It's not surprising that hikers and campers go missing and are murdered," I say. "They're in vulnerable positions in secluded places—which attracts predators."

"Of course," he says. "And it's always been that way, you're right, but it's happening at an alarming rate—much higher than you would think, at a much higher percentage per capita than it should be."

"That doesn't explain why you're here," I say.

"Research," he says. "Investigation."

"When someone goes missing or is found murdered in a national or state park or on a hiking trail or at a place like this," I say, "you show up and investigate, right?"

"Right. I'm the only one who is," he says. "Who's seeing the links, connecting the dots."

"Then tell me how it is that you showed up here well in advance of the bodies being discovered."

"I didn't," he says. "I mean . . . I didn't come up here knowing two bodies would be found, but I . . . follow patterns. I knew a body would be found somewhere in this region of North Florida. I just didn't know it would be here—in this exact location. The truth is . . . I was here to do a little throwaway segment on the Bigfoot sighting while waiting for the next murder victim to turn up."

"Bigfoot?"

"Look, that kind of shit—anything uncanny or paranormal —that's what pays the bills. I do it to fund my investigation.

That's the only reason I do it. I'm a cop. Like you. And I'm investigating one of the greatest hidden and unsolved cases in American history. There are several vicious, prolific serial killers working the parks, campgrounds, and hiking trails of our country and no one's even aware. They're killing with impunity. There's never been anything like it."

I don't doubt there are serial killers using rural and secluded areas to hunt and hide their victims, but I highly doubt it's to the extent he's claiming. Far more likely, as in the case of the Atlanta Child Murders task force, he's conveniently attributing victims to a single serial killer or a small group of serial killers because they were killed or dumped near where the actual series victims were found. It's lazy investigative work.

"Are you saying you believe both the victims discovered here were killed by a serial killer?" I ask.

"I'm not saying anything that definitively," he says. "But what *I am* saying—and what you can't afford to ignore—is both of them fit into a certain established pattern."

"You believe the same serial killer murdered these two victims?" I ask.

"That's not what I said."

"Or, even more incredibly, that this small campground on the outskirts of this small town, has been the killing ground for two different serial killers?"

"You're trying to put words in my mouth. That's not what I said. You arrogant, know-it-all pricks are all alike. All I'm saying is each murder—individually, respectively—fits a certain pattern of other victims found in public parks just like this one. Hell, I'll do your damn job for you and give you copies of the cases."

"I would really appreciate that very much," I say. "And I promise to look at it carefully and thoroughly with an open mind and not to remain an arrogant, know-it-all prick my entire life."

35

While I wait for Captain Jack to retrieve copies of case files for me out of his camper, Evelyn Hillman comes up to me.

"How goes the investigation?" she asks.

"Slower than we'd like," I say.

"Not quick and easy like on TV, is it?"

"Nothing is," I say. "Can't really remodel a house or solve a murder in less than an hour."

"Fifty minutes with commercials," she says. "Ain't it the truth? Well, there's a bit of scuttlebutt floating about that might help."

"Oh yeah? What's that?"

"Word around the campground is that Melissa Tate—that's the wife in that sweet little Sunseeker RV over in sixteen—was having an affair with the victim."

"Which one?" I ask.

"Oh, the man from the picnic table, of course, but how PC of you to ask. No, Chris Taunton."

"Did you ever see them together or him hanging out over there or anything?"

"We should ask HC and Georgia about that," she says. "The thing is Melissa and Channing—that's her husband—are swingers. Several couples who live the campers' lifestyle are, but . . . Well. . . Seems as though some of the men Mrs. Tate has been seeing are or were single. It ain't swinging if it's not another couple, you ask me, it's just an affair. And they say she does a lot of solo swinging. Now, look, I don't want anyone knowing this came from me—especially this part I'm about to tell you. I'm just telling you so you'll know what's being talked and you can look into it for yourself if you want to. Okay?"

"Okay."

"As I said, Melissa is, ah, active. Very active from what I understand. I don't know how much of it is true or not, but . . . he does stop in a lot over there when he's making his rounds."

"Who?"

"Deputy Cody Faircloth," she says. "They say he's carrying on a little solo swinging with Mrs. Tate too. It's funny . . . Everybody thinks it's a cop, but what if they're right and wrong. What if instead of you it's Deputy Faircloth?"

Before I can respond, she turns her attention away from me and begins motioning for HC and Georgia to join us.

They don't look happy about it, but they amble over to us.

"Who do we have here?" Evelyn says.

She's talking about the baby that the middle-aged woman is holding, but HC introduces everyone. "This is my son, Carter, Jr., and his wife, Dallas, their daughter, Patricia, and granddaughter little April."

Carter, Jr., and Dallas look awkward and uncomfortable and aren't particularly friendly. Patricia is younger and sadder than she had looked from a distance. Or maybe it's anger instead of sadness. It's hard to tell. The only pleasantness any of them emit is toward April.

"She's a precious little thing," Evelyn says.

"Thank you," Georgia says. "We certainly think so, but I'm sure we're biased."

"Well," HC says, "we better head back over to our place. These people are anxious to get on the road. Had about as much Dead Lakes Campground excitement as they can take for one day."

"Just have one quick question for you," she says.

"Okay," he says. "Georgia, why don't you take them on over there so they can get everything ready and I'll be right behind you?"

Without saying anything, they turn and begin walking toward the host camper.

"Nice to meet y'all," Evelyn says. "You have a beautiful family, HC."

"Thank you, Evelyn. Now, what can I do for you?"

"What can you tell the detective here about Melissa Tate's involvement with the victim and Deputy Faircloth?"

"What?" he asks, his expression showing his obvious distaste. "Nothing. I'm not gonna spread gossip about guests here."

"Not gossip," she says. "Did you ever see either of them over there at their RV?"

"A few times, so what? I've been over there too. What does that prove?"

"You saw both Chris Taunton and Cody Faircloth in the Tate's RV repeatedly?" I ask.

"Yeah, so what? What does it prove?"

"That they knew each other," I say. "Something they didn't indicate when they gave their statement."

36

M elissa Tate is a petite young woman whose diminutive stature makes her look even younger than she is. Her husband, Channing, is a huge, older man with a long, full gray beard and big beefy hands.

She's in her twenties but could pass for a teenager. He's in his fifties but looks mid-sixties.

She's wearing extremely small, extremely short cutoffs and a bikini top that reveals she has large, protruding nipples and virtually no breasts. He's wearing jeans and a wife beater, his large belly framed by the narrow straps of his red suspenders.

Their RV smells of sweat, testosterone, and sex.

"What can we do you for, officer?" Channing asks. "You want a beer or a soda or something?"

He doesn't look like a Channing.

"I'm good, thanks."

Melissa is sitting on a bench, her feet propped up on the removable dining table. Legs spread, feet apart, magazine on the table between them, she is painting her toenails and looking at the pictures of celebrities.

"I'm here to conduct a follow-up with you regarding the

initial statement you gave to the deputy that interviewed you," I say.

"Sure thing," Channing says. "How can we help?"

"Tell me what you can about either of the victims," I say.

"Never heard who the girl was," he says, "but based on the description . . . Don't think we ever met her. I guess it's possible that we did and don't remember or . . . But until we know who she is or see a picture or something . . . 'fraid we can't help you there."

"Same go for you, Miss?" I say.

She nods.

"It's *Mrs.*," Channing says.

"Sorry."

"No problem."

I'm looking at Channing, who is sitting in a recliner, which he dwarfs, but can see Melissa out of the corner of my eye. It seems everything she does is sexual, seductive—self-consciously so. The way she has her legs spread. The way she has her feet up on the table. The way she leans forward to look at the magazine and paint her nails. It's as if before each act she asks herself what is the most sensual and provocative way this can be done?

"What about the other victim?" I ask. "Chris Taunton. What can you tell me about him?"

Channing shrugs. "Not a lot I'm afraid. Didn't know him that well."

"Oh really? Because we have witness statements that say he spent a good bit of time over here."

"Wouldn't say a good bit, but some, sure. Don't mean we knew him very well."

"What was your relationship with him like?"

"*Relationship*? Didn't have a *relationship*. He hung out a few times. Had a few beers. That's about it."

"How'd you meet? Where did you know him from?"

"I keep tellin' you . . . We didn't know him. We have . . . like this open door policy. Ours is sort of known as the party place of this campground. We hang out, drink, shoot the shit, do adult stuff. People show up. Like I said it's an open door kind of situation. We assume it's mostly other campers who join in, but word gets out and . . . we get a few folks from town too."

"Like Cody Faircloth?" I ask.

"Who?"

"The deputy," Melissa says without looking up.

"Oh. Yeah. He hangs sometimes. It's all very informal. Casual. HC and Georgia are here some too. People come and go —in the park, in our home."

"Did either of you see Chris on the day he was killed?"

He shakes his head. "I didn't. How about you, honey?"

She shakes her head without looking up.

"Can y'all think of anyone who would want to kill him?"

"You mean besides you?" Melissa asks, this time looking up and locking eyes with me.

"Yeah. Besides me."

She smiles and gives me a wink.

"Did y'all ever see him arguing or fighting with anyone? Did he have any conflict with anyone you know of?"

They both shake their heads.

"Earlier you mentioned you do *adult stuff* at your gatherings," I say. "What did you mean?"

"My wife and I like to fuck," Channing says. "We hang out with people who like to fuck. And we fuck."

"Were either of you involved in a sexual relationship with the victim?" I ask.

"We have an open marriage, and we swing," Channing says, "but this old barn door only swings one way. I'm as heterosexual as they come. I'm sure Melissa fucked him a time or two at some of our parties."

Melissa shrugs. "Think so. One night about a month ago we

had an orgy. Think pretty much everybody had a go at her that night. I'm pretty sure what's his face Chris was here for that one."

"Did Chris ever cross any lines? Make anyone angry or jealous? Or—"

"It's just sex," Channing says. "Laid back. Relaxed. Everyone's chill about it. No conflict. No drama. I assure you whatever got him killed it wasn't dipping his wick at one of our little parties."

37

Later that evening, I'm studying Chris's phone logs and the case materials Captain Jack gave me at the kitchen table when Cody Faircloth rings our doorbell.

He's in uniform, and over his shoulder, I can see that his car is idling in the driveway, the radio blaring from inside audible from the slightly open driver's side door.

"Hey, John," he says, his tone warm and friendly as if we're buddies. "You got a minute?"

"What's up?" I say.

"You mind stepping out here with me for a moment?"

I look over my shoulder at Anna, who is working on her laptop at the kitchen table. "I'm gonna step outside with Deputy Faircloth a moment," I say. "Be back in a minute."

After I've closed the door behind me and we've stepped into the yard a few feet, he says, "Melissa said you interviewed her this evening."

I nod.

"Said you asked about Chris and about me."

I nod again.

"Why didn't you just ask me?"

"I plan on it," I say. "But I was gonna have Reggie and the lieutenant present when I did it."

"Why? You don't need to involve them. Don't make a big deal out of nothin'. That's a waste of everybody's time. I'll tell you anything you want to know. Just ask."

"It's for your protection more than anything else," I say. "You'll have the option of having a union rep present, and we'll record it, so—"

"Because I've been to a few parties at the Tates'? That's nuts. Why're you making such a thing of this? It's nothing."

"You and the victim were having a sexual relationship with the same woman," I say. "Neither you nor the woman, who you interviewed, disclosed this to anyone. We'll talk about why with Reggie and the lieutenant present."

"Oh, now I see what you're doin'," he says. "I get it now. You're tryin' to deflect suspicion off you and your family and friends and onto me and Melissa. I see what you're doin'. Well, let me tell you something, I'm not a motherfucker you want to mess with. You understand me? If you want to pin this shit on someone, pin it on someone else. Not me. Not Melissa. I know you're smart and all, but you aren't street tough and you don't want to mess with someone who is. Understand? Don't invite my kind of trouble into your life. It ain't worth it."

He pauses, but I just hold his gaze without saying anything.

It's not lost on me that he has shown up to my house armed and on duty.

"I hope I'm getting through to you," he says. "I really do. But let's put all of that aside for a minute, okay? Listen carefully to what I'm about to say. Melissa Tate is a truly sweet girl. I've never met anyone with more love to give."

I'm tempted to make a crack about that, but I refrain.

"She's a true innocent," he continues. "A lover, not a fighter. She wouldn't hurt anyone. Come after me if you want to, though I seriously wouldn't advise it, but don't you go after her.

Leave her out of all this. You hear me? Leave her out of this or I won't just bring the house down around you, I'll fuck with someone you care about."

"Get in your car, Cody, and get off my property and don't ever come back here again. Not for any reason. I take threats to my loved ones very seriously. You just crossed a line you can't come back from. If you don't leave right now or if you ever come back I'm going to treat you like a threat to my family and—"

"And what? Do to me what y'all did to Chris? Good fuckin' luck with that, you arrogant motherfucker. Good fuckin' luck with that."

I stand in my yard, watching Cody back down my driveway and ease down my road, waiting until he turns onto Highway 22 and disappears before going back inside.

"What was that about?" Anna asks.

I sit back down across the kitchen table from her and tell her.

"Clearly he has something to hide," she says. "But what? Is it his extracurricular activities or more?"

"That *is* the question," I say. "Whether 'tis nobler in the mind to suffer the slings and arrows of outrageous fortune . . . Let's be extra careful until we find out just how desperate he is."

"We've taken up arms against a sea of troubles before," she says. "We can do it again. But I'd feel better if you'd tell Reggie about it all sooner rather than later."

"You got it," I say. "I'll talk to her tonight."

"Where are you getting with the phone records and case files?"

I glance back down at Chris's call log. "There are a few numbers we still haven't identified. We got him calling you a lot, mostly early in the afternoon-evening, then both his parents later that night. We've got you calling him back. Both of them calling him back. Then we've got him calling another number we can't trace and him receiving two calls we can't trace."

"Probably prepaid burner phones," she says.

"But one of the numbers is vaguely familiar to me," I say. "It's the next to the last call too. There's a period of time before it comes when he doesn't make or receive any calls. After you call him back, there's nearly an hour. Then he starts calling his folks. Has a few conversations with them, then nothing for a while. Then one more call from his mom about an hour later. Then nothing for about twenty-five minutes, then he calls this unknown number, then he gets a call, then nothing for another half an hour or so, then he gets this last call an hour or so later. The final call was very brief, just thirty-six seconds, but I wonder if it was the killer, confirming his whereabouts."

"Sounds like it," she says.

"I keep calling it, but so far no answer, and there's no voice-mail set up on it. Maybe if we narrow down our suspects some more, we'll find it on one of them."

"Maybe so."

"You ready to tell me what you talked to Chris about that night?" I ask.

"You heard what I told Tony," she says.

"Yes, I did," I say. "And my question still stands."

"Don't ask if you don't want to know," she says.

"I'd rather know than not," I say. "Always. No matter what the truth is, I'd rather know."

"I talked to him about something I haven't even talked to you about yet."

"*Really*?" I ask, willing myself to remain calm, telling myself to hear what she has to say before reacting, reminding myself not to overreact no matter what she says.

"I was always going to," she says. "But then the bottom dropped out, and I just haven't yet."

"Until Chris's death I'd've said we didn't keep anything from each other," I say. "Not anything that really matters."

"I think that's true," she says. "It was true, and it still is. Like I said, I was always going to tell you, but when I found out you were working the Mariah Evers case and then you had to go back to Atlanta, and then all this happened. The thing is . . . Usually, you're with me at the doctor appointments, and if you would have been this time, you would've heard it when I did."

"Heard what?"

"The two words Taylor's pediatrician spoke that made me know with absolute certainty Chris had to die."

"What two words?" I ask.

"Developmental delay."

38

"Because of his affairs, Chris gave me an STD," she says. "I was humiliated. I was heartbroken. I was angry, but I didn't want to kill him. I left him. I found more happiness than I thought was possible and then I got the abnormal pap smear back. Remember? The HPV he had given me had turned into cervical cancer, and I had to have embarrassing and humiliating and painful procedures, and even as I did, even as I loathed him for his weakness and deceit and duplicity, I didn't want to kill him. And then he tried to have you killed, and in the process nearly had me and the baby killed. He didn't tell the madman to beat me up and stomp my pregnant belly, but he set everything into motion that led to that. All three of us almost died—you, me, and Taylor—but when they rushed me into surgery and saved the baby, and everything was okay, and then we found out he was behind it, I wanted him in prison, I wanted him punished for what he had done, I wanted him off the street, but I didn't want to kill him. Then he got out, and he started stalking me and harassing us, even broke into our home with a gun and held us hostage, and I wanted him out of our lives, wanted him in custody, but I didn't want to kill him. But when Dr. Ibid said Taylor had developmental delays, when she confirmed what I already knew—that the beating I had suffered at the hands of Chris's hired madmen had done damage to our daughter, I knew he had to die."

I jump up and rush around the table and hug her. I wanted to do it sooner but didn't want to break her flow, to interrupt her when she was sharing such painful memories, confiding such embarrassing intimacies.

The entire time she has talked, she has been calm, mostly matter-of-fact, but now that I'm holding her, she breaks down and begins to sob.

Though I can't know for sure, I get the sense she's crying about Taylor's condition more than anything else, that actually saying it out loud to me has made it more real somehow.

"You . . . understand. . . Don't you?" she says.

"Of course."

"I knew you would," she says. "I never doubted that, not for . . . a single . . . second. What mother wouldn't want to kill with her bare hands the man who damaged her child? Oh my God, John . . . our baby. Can you believe she's got . . . that . . . because of what that monster did . . . she's . . ."

"It's going to be okay," I say. "She's going to be fine. We'll do everything we can to help her, spend every dime we ever make on getting her the best treatment and care and . . . whatever she needs."

"His own daughter," she says. "I'm so glad he's dead. The world is better without him in it."

I nod and wipe the tears from her cheeks with my fingertips.

"Would you mind grabbing me a glass of water and some tissue?" she asks.

"Of course not," I say, and move off to do it.

I return a few moments later with ice water and a box of

tissues and wait while she sips the water and dabs the corners of her eyes.

"I'm sorry I didn't tell you sooner," she says. "I was going to. I was going to tell you all of it as soon as you got back from Atlanta—tell you what he had done to our daughter, tell you I couldn't abide him walking around drawing breath after what he had done or caused such a thing to be done, but then Reggie called and said he was dead and I was just so relieved he was dead, and then the investigation started, and I kept thinking it had to be Merrill or your dad and I was just so . . . and then Carla told us what she did that first night about wanting us to adopt her child, and everything has been happening so fast."

"You don't actually know who killed him?" I say.

"Not for sure, no," she says. "But Merrill and your dad saw how upset I was, heard me say that he had hurt us beyond what anyone knew, heard me say how he was never going to leave us alone until he killed us or died himself. Merrill was up there at the park that night. And when I went back later . . . I saw your dad's truck. He was up there too that night. And neither of them came back to our house to watch us or check on us—had to be because they knew the threat was gone, right?"

I thought about dad's swollen knuckles, about how he and Merrill had been acting.

"So what did you tell him on the phone?" I ask. "Why did you really go back up there?"

"I taunted him, John. Told him what a piece of shit he was for harming his own daughter. Told him the only reason he wouldn't kill himself is that he's such a weak coward. I called him out. Told him I was going to tell the whole world what a terrible human being he was. Then I told him I was taking the girls to the park to play if he was man enough to try to finish the job his criminal friends had started. I went armed. I had that little 9mm in my purse, and I was just hoping he'd attack me so I could be the one to end him right there in the open for everyone to see. But he never did. I knew he was there watching, but he never came at me. When we got home I thought well, maybe he didn't want to do it in front of his daughter, so I left the girls with the babysitter and went back, just me, hoping he'd come out and attack me since I was by myself, but . . . he didn't, and now I think he was already dead or at least in the process of being beaten to death by then. But . . . I can't let Merrill or your dad be arrested for doing what I should've done, what I wanted to do, what I set up to happen. He was there because I called him out, I taunted and belittled him. That's on me."

"No," I say. "It's on me. I'm the one who should've handled this better from the very beginning. It wasn't your job or Merrill's or Dad's or anyone else's. It was mine. I should have been protecting my family better."

"You kept us completely safe," she says. "We're all fine. None of this is on you. I brought all this into your life, all of it."

"No, you didn't," I say. "The only person responsible for what Chris has done is Chris. But I should have done a better job of taking care of you and Taylor—even back before she was born. I should have done more to protect you on that blood moon night at the prison. I should have been smarter about working the case against him. It was my fault it was tossed out. And I certainly shouldn't have let this go on as long as it did. It's my fault. It's on me. And I'm not going to let Merrill or Dad or anyone else take the fall for something that should've never happened in the first place."

"What're you gonna do?" she asks. "You can't take the blame for something you didn't do. You can't—"

My phone starts buzzing on the table, and I can see that it's Bobby Ink.

"Take it," she says. "Maybe he has word for you about the female victim."

"Hey Bobby," I say as I answer it.

"Who's your favorite Native-African-American tattoo artist?" he asks.

"You are," I say. "It's not even close."

"I tracked down the ID of your victim for you," he says. "Found the artist who did her ink and got a copy of her paperwork. I'm looking at her information right now."

39

H er name was Rebecca Blackburn. She was seventeen years old. And she gave this life far more than it ever gave her.

Genuinely kind, she had been the kind of pretty and popular girl who was nice to everyone in her high school—no matter their socio-economic level.

The following morning I drive up Highway 231 to what can only be described as her family's compound—a farm with several old mobile homes and campers on it surrounded by a high privacy fence made of vertical standing roofing tin.

When I first arrive, I'm greeted with suspicion, but when I show my badge, it turns into contempt.

Unwilling to allow me into any of the structures, Rebecca Blackburn's parents, Timothy and Esther, meet with me near my car, as other adults look on from the stoops and stairs of their campers and mobile homes.

"Have you found her?" Esther asks. "Is she okay?"

"There is only one question," Timothy says. "Is she ready to repent and return?"

Timothy and Esther Blackburn look far older than what

they really are, the burden of their humorless, rigid religion like a death shroud hanging over them. They are dressed in plain, ill-fitting clothes and their longish, jagged haircuts look to have been done by a child.

"Is this your daughter?" I ask, showing them a picture printed from her Facebook page.

"Yes, that's Rebecca," Esther says.

"No," Timothy says. "That was our daughter, but she turned her back on her family and her faith and is dead to us until she repents her sins and submits to the discipline of the community. There are no exceptions—no more for my family than anyone else's."

"When is the last time you saw or spoke to her?" I ask.

"Two months, two weeks, and three days," Esther says.

"Did you report her missing?" I ask.

"I wanted to," Esther says.

"She wasn't missing," Timothy says. "She was lost in sin, seduced by Satan. She made a choice to turn her back on God and have intercourse with the world. It all started when she insisted on leaving the spiritual instruction of homeschool and attending the devil's workshop down the road."

"She's extremely intelligent," Esther says. "She wanted to study things I couldn't teach her—complex chemistry and foreign languages and . . . She just wanted to develop the amazing mind God gave her."

"Forsaking the God of her youth and going to that vile place is what started her on this path of destruction," Timothy says. "I have tasks I must do. Esther, you may answer a few more questions but be quick about it. I've told you . . . until she repents and returns, we're not throwin' any more good effort after foolishness."

With that, he turns and walks away.

"He's not as harsh as he sounds," she says. "He's hurt.

Rebecca is his favorite. Always has been. She broke his heart when she . . ."

"When she what?"

"Went to the outside school, then . . . wound up pregnant. He sent her away in her shame."

"To have the baby?"

"He prayed about it, and God told him she would lose it, that it wasn't a blessed child, but . . . I don't know. I thought maybe . . . God would turn it around and make what the devil meant for bad into something good. Eventually, she came back."

"With or without her baby?" I ask.

"Without. She wouldn't talk about it. She just said it was taken care of. I thought she had . . . aborted it and didn't want to talk about it, which was okay with me. I was just glad to have her back. I thought she was doing real well. She seemed to be. Was back in homeschool. Submissive again. Seemed like her old sweet self, just a little sadder, but . . . then . . . she just . . . disappeared one day. Just up and left in the middle of the night."

"Two months, two weeks, and three days ago," I say.

"Yes. Why are you here? Have you found her? Where is she? Is she in jail? Did something happen? Did she have an illegal back-alley abortion?"

"Mrs. Blackburn, I'm afraid I have some very, very bad news," I say. "I'm very sorry, but we've found the body of a young woman we believe to be your daughter."

She collapses to the ground screaming "Noooooo."

I kneel down beside her and put my hand on her shoulder as what seems like the entire community rushes over to us.

"Get your hand off another man's wife," one of the men shouts at me as he runs up.

"What is it?" one of the women asks Esther. "What's happened?"

When Timothy reaches us, he looks at me and says, "Is she dead? Did she die in her sin?"

"We're waiting for positive identification, but we found the body of a young woman we believe to be Rebecca."

"How did she die?" he yells to be heard over the lamentations of his wife. "How did the devil kill my little girl?"

"We believe she was murdered," I say. "I'm very sorry."

"Don't be," he says, turning his head slightly and raising his voice even more. "That's what the devil does." He's talking for the benefit of the community now. "The wages of sin is death, but the gift of God is eternal life. What does the devil reward you for a life of sin with? Death and decay. Murder."

40

"I just can't believe she's dead," Kay Brooks says.

"She can't be," Megan Waller says. "She just can't be."

I'm at the Devil's Workshop public school—though that's not the name they use for it—talking to Rebecca's favorite teacher and best friend.

Kay Brooks, the reading teacher, is a thirty-something, brown-eyed natural beauty who wears no makeup and spends no time on her hair except to pull it into a ponytail. She, like Rebecca's classmate and best friend, Megan, is sniffing and wiping away tears.

"It's a case of her truly being too good for this world," Kay says. "I've never met a more thoughtful or considerate teenager."

"She really was the sweetest," Megan says. "Though how she could be, coming from that crazy religious cult family, I don't know."

"Do you know who the father of her baby was?" I ask Megan.

She shrugs. "Not really. Not for sure."

"She had a boyfriend, didn't she?" Kay says.

"Yeah. Jarred Martin."

"Was it his?" I ask.

Kay says, "I always thought so."

"It could've been, but . . . I don't know," Megan says. "He's a good guy. A really good guy. I think if it were his he would've stepped up and—but they broke up and when it was obvious she was pregnant they didn't get back together or anything."

"There was talk," Kay says, "about one of the coaches being too close to Rebecca."

"Coach Carroll, yeah," Megan says. "He teaches civics and coaches softball. I told her to keep her distance from him, but she'd just say he was sweet and harmless. She was pretty naive."

"She was very smart, but had been very sheltered for a very long time," Kay says. "And she was trusting in that way that only truly trustworthy and genuinely good people can be—especially those who are young and inexperienced."

"Do you think it's possible she was having an affair with Coach Carroll?" I ask.

"He has a reputation," Kay says. "But his entire family's in the school system, and his uncle is the superintendent of schools, so . . . he's pretty protected. I've complained to our principal that he's too casual, too familiar, with the kids—especially the girls, but to my knowledge, nothing was ever done."

"It's like school shootings," Megan says, "those who can and should do something, don't. The ones with the real power who are supposed to be protecting us and taking care of us just don't. It's like they really don't give a fuck about us."

Instead of reacting to Megan's use of the word *fuck*, Kay just nods her enthusiastic agreement.

"It's true," Kay says. "In some ways, we're all sitting ducks, but in others, some among us are especially vulnerable. And the powers that be don't seem to give a . . . *fuck*."

I nod and think about how often the greed and selfishness

and self-interests of those in positions of power and responsibility prevent them from doing even the bare basics of their sacred trusts.

I look at Megan. "Do you know what happened with Rebecca's pregnancy? Her mother seems to think she may have terminated it."

"No way. Never. She was . . . She had already gone through the worst part of losing everything—her reputation, her chance at graduating here, her family. She said she was going to keep it."

"Do you know if she did?"

"No, I don't know for sure what happened," Megan says. "We lost touch. She said she was gonna take care of everything and she'd get in touch with me when she got back, but . . . I never heard from her again. I tried to find her. Went out to her folks' farm, but they wouldn't let me in and wouldn't tell me anything. Said it was loose girls like me that was the reason she got pregnant in the first place."

"Do you know if she had the baby or what might have happened?" I ask Kay.

"I know she intended to, but I also know she was having some complications with her pregnancy, so . . . she may have—could her death be the result of her delivery?"

I shake my head. "She wasn't pregnant when she was killed. Do you know when she was due?"

"April twelfth," Megan says. "On my birthday."

We had found Rebecca's body in July, and she had been killed sometime in May, so whatever happened with her baby happened at least a month before that. Maybe longer.

"I got the sense she didn't plan on involving the father," Kay says. "And that she was going to put her baby up for adoption. Of course, that doesn't mean he didn't find out or that the complications she was having didn't take the decision to have it out of her hands, but..."

"And you're both pretty sure the father had to either be Jarred Martin or Coach Carroll?" I ask. "She wasn't involved with anyone else?"

"I don't think she ever got involved with him," Megan says, "cause I think he creeped her out, but there was this guy who started putting the full-court pressure on her at the Wewa football game."

"Do you know his name?"

She shakes her head. "And like I said, she wasn't interested. He came on strong, and that didn't work on her."

"Do you remember what he looked like or anything about him?"

"No, I didn't see him. I was cheering," she says. "Sorry. No, wait. I'm ... Give me just a ... I'm pretty sure he said he was a cop because that freaked her out a little. And he had one of those names ... You know ... The way he acted fit his name ... What was it? You know like Tyler or Trevor. What was it? You know the type. Oh. Cody. It was Cody."

41

I'm on my way back to meet with Reggie and the other investigators about Cody Faircloth and the other recent evidence we've all turned up when Carla calls.

"Hey John," she says.

"How are you?" I ask. "How're you feeling?"

"I'm okay. Are you mad at me?"

"No," I say. "Not at all. What makes you ask that?"

"Because of what I'm doing," she says. "Because I wasn't honest with you about it."

"I'm not mad at you," I say. "I understand how challenging all this is."

"I still want you and Anna to adopt my baby," she says.

"We still want to," I say, "but it's got to be okay with the father too."

"But if I tell him, there's a chance Rick will find out," she says. "That's my fiancé's name."

"I think you should tell them both," I say. "Be honest with everyone involved. You owe it to the father, and you don't want to start your marriage keeping secrets like this from your husband."

"I just can't. You don't understand. It's just not possible. Please, just this once . . . for me . . . Please. Don't do the right thing. Just this once. For me. It's not like I'm asking for some big bad thing."

"You don't think I understand?" I say.

"How could you, really?" she says.

"I'll tell you how. Do you know how long Susan kept Johanna a secret from me? Do you know how unfair that was—to me and to Johanna? Do you remember how much time I missed? How many years? How sad that made me—still makes me? I can't get any of that time back. Susan made a decision that impacted my life in the hugest way possible and never told me, and it's the single worst thing anyone has ever done to me in my entire life. No father should ever have to experience that. No child either. So I understand far better than you think."

"I meant from my perspective, from the mother's point of view," she says. "Besides, my baby's biological father is not you, John. He's nothing like you. He won't care. He'll be as glad to get rid of the baby as he was me. You can't judge the rest of the world based on what you would do or how you would feel. You're . . . He's nothing like you."

"If you don't think he'll want the baby, then you have nothing to fear from telling him," I say. "Just come clean—the way you did with Anna and me. It'll—"

"I just can't, John. I understand why you can't adopt him under these circumstances, but please understand why I can't do what you're asking. I'll have to find someone else to adopt my baby. Goodbye, John. Please forgive me. I hope someday you'll understand."

After she ends the call, I call Anna.

"I just spoke with Carla," I say.

"And?"

"She's not willing to tell the biological father," I say. "Says she just can't."

"Maybe she'll change her mind once she thinks about it some more."

"Maybe, but I don't think we can count on that."

"No, I agree, we can't."

"She should tell the father," I say.

"I know."

"We're right to insist that she does," I say.

"I know."

"But . . . if you want to adopt him anyway, I'm willing to."

"You are?"

"I am."

"Are you sure?" she asks.

"Positive. I'm pulling up to the sheriff's office now. We can talk about it more tonight, but the decision is yours. I'll go with whatever you decide."

"But—"

"I will," I say. "And I'll never give it a second thought."

"Now I know you're lying," she says.

I laugh. "Well, I'll never mention it again."

"Thank you, John. I know what it means, know what you're doing and why."

"Oh yeah? Why's that?"

"You love me more than your convictions and principles," she says. "Which is another way of saying you love me more than yourself."

42

"We've got to look at the boyfriend—What's his name? Jarred Martin—and the coach, but we've got to take a very hard look at Cody Faircloth too," Reggie is saying.

We are in her office—me, Jessica Young, Tony Ford, Darlene Weatherly, and Arnie Ward, who has just returned to work after eye surgery.

I've just shared with them what Kay and Megan told me.

"If we can find the baby—or the fetus, if she didn't carry it to term," Jessica says, "we can determine paternity through DNA. If we can get the three guys to submit swabs."

"Speaking of DNA," Reggie says. "You know how behind FDLE is and how we're still waiting for all our labs? They got a grant from the justice department to use private labs to catch up, so we'll be getting all our results back sooner than expected."

"That's great news," Jessica says.

"Yes, it is," Tony says. "Thank you, Uncle Sam."

"The lieutenant and I are going to interview Faircloth tomorrow," Reggie says. "Let me know anything specific you want covered. I think we have to consider him a potential suspect and or witness on both cases. Everyone look out for each other and watch your backs. If he was making threats before, no telling how he's gonna respond to being questioned and possibly suspended, pending the investigation."

She pauses, but no one says anything.

"How are we coming on other fronts?" she asks.

I tell them about what Captain Jack said and the cases he gave me copies of.

"Anything in it?" Reggie asks.

"I'm still going through them. Hope to finish tonight. So far I'm not seeing a pattern that connects them. They're all over the place in terms of age and race and size and hair and eye color. The only thing that might possibly link some of them are the locations where they were found, manner and cause of death, and the way the bodies were disposed of. But only a few have all three things in common. I'll see what else I can find, but it's not looking particularly promising. He is right about one thing, though. We've got way too many unsolved homicides in our state and national parks. If there is some sort of pattern, I hope we can find it."

"We should all take a look at it," Darlene says. "The more eyes, the better. I'll give them a look after you finish."

"Sounds good. Thanks."

"What else?" Reggie says.

"Things are progressing in our case too," Tony says. "We've been looking into the victim's financial dealings, following the money. I've got a couple of FDLE analysts trying to trace the cash and looking into some of his old clients and his previous partners and their firm. It's early days, but they've already found some anomalies, so . . . that could be promising."

"Great. What else?"

Darlene says, "We've been looking into an old case against Chris that fell apart. He had been having an affair with a young woman in Tallahassee named Ashley Fountain. He set up a guy named Ronnie Cardigan. Shot and killed another young man named Karl Jason."

I had told Darlene about the case and how it might be a good idea to look into everyone connected, but until this moment I didn't know she had.

"We thought it would be a good idea to look at all the people Chris has crossed or killed or destroyed in some way," she continues. "Look at them—the ones that are still alive—or their families to see if Chris's murder could be retribution for something he's done."

"That's a great idea," Reggie says.

"It was all hers," Tony says.

"Anyway, it's a long list and it's taking some time, but it's showing some promise. I should have more to share by the end of the week."

"Nice work, Darlene," Reggie says. "First class police work."

"Thank you, but it's all just a team effort. We're also taking a very close look at Randa Raffield," she adds. "Supposedly she was in a holding cell in the Gulf County jail instead of in the Liberty County jail where she should have been when Chris was killed."

"Really?" Arnie says. "That's got to move her to the top of the suspect list, doesn't it? Security in the jail here is a joke."

Tony nods. "We've got a lot of promising suspects. Like Darlene said there's no shortage of people with motives. This prick was a piece of work. We've still got the Raffield woman on the list, but she's got a lot of company. We're not ready to rule anyone out just yet."

"Because we've found a connection between our two victims," Reggie says. "I think we've got to consider the very real possibility that the same killer or killers were involved in both crimes. I know we've had it as a possibility we were open to, but the fact that Faircloth and maybe even the couple— what're their names? The Tates—could be tied to both of them, means there's actually a good chance they are connected."

Everyone nods but Tony Ford.

"I want you all to coordinate even more and communicate with each other more—especially in those areas where the two homicide victims or their lives intersect."

"I have to say, I don't think that's a good idea," Tony says. "I think to maintain the integrity of our case we have to keep it separate from the other one."

"Why's that?"

"You're putting me in an incredibly difficult situation here, but I'm just gonna say it and let the chips fall where they may. I haven't ruled out Investigator Jordan as a suspect in my case." He looks over at me. "No offense. I'm just being honest. I'm not accusing you of anything, but . . . If we're gonna sit in here and say Deputy Faircloth is a suspect we have to have the integrity to say you are a suspect."

I nod. "I agree."

He looks back at Reggie. "And do you know who I suspect even more than John? His wife and father and some of his other friends. It was a mistake to assign him to the Rebecca Blackburn case—especially if the two cases are connected. Don't compound that mistake by folding these two investigations into one another."

When he finishes, no one says anything. Reggie looks at me.

"You can send me back to Tallahassee if you want to," Tony says, "but that'll only make you all look like you're covering up for someone you know. And I'm afraid if you do—especially with the noise Lyle Taunton is making and the suits he's filing —eventually, the governor will be forced to call for an independent, outside investigation, and if something like that happens, you could all be indicted—for obstruction and conspiracy if nothing else."

43

"I really don't want to lose my job," Tad Barnes says. "Decent job's hard to come by in this little town, and I like this one. And believe it or not, I'm pretty good at it."

Darlene and I are talking with the correctional officer in charge of Randa Raffield's custody the night Chris was killed.

He asked us to meet him as far away from the jail as we could so no one would see us talking to him.

We are at the April Bennet Memorial Garden inside the Remington James Wildlife Sanctuary where Anna and I and our girls have just taken a walk and watered and weeded a few of the flower beds—something we do about once a week as part of our commitment to and stewardship over this sacred place.

Anna continues to weed one of the beds, as the girls play nearby, while Darlene and I talk to Tad.

"We're not looking to cost you your job," Darlene says.

"But if it gets out that I . . ."

"We'll try our best to keep it just between us," I say. "Just tell us what happened that night."

"Well . . . The thing is . . . we ain't used to havin' any women there—not very often anyway—and we ain't used to having anybody up in that front holding cell at night."

"We know," Darlene says. "It's an unusual situation, easy for unusual things to happen."

"She was such a nice, mannerly lady," he says. "Most of the women we get are crack whores, all strung out and shit, but this was a very classy woman—smart, polite, respectful, nice. She didn't cause me a second of trouble. My policy is the Golden Rule. You treat me with respect, I'm gonna treat you with respect."

"And that's what you did," Darlene says.

"Yeah. She said she gets claustrophobic could I please leave the cell door open . . . and . . . well . . . the thing is the outside doors are locked, so she's still locked in, what does it matter her cell door is open, right?"

Darlene and I both nod, as if we agree.

"So I left it open."

Which means there was only a single door between Randa Raffield and the outside world.

"Did you see her go out of her cell at any time?" Darlene asks.

"We had sixteen inmates in the back, and we were short-handed that night," he says. "Sixteen inmates in the open bay dorm. They required our attention and our . . . The thing is . . . I'm not used to havin' someone up in that front holding cell. I got called to the back. Couple of inmates were fighting, and well, I stayed back there because I . . . the truth is . . . I forgot we had somebody in that front cell."

"How long were you gone?" I ask.

"Most of my shift. Settled everyone down. Ate my dinner. Did lights out. And then in the middle of the night, I'm sitting there, and it hits me. Shit! We've got an inmate up front. So I go and check on her."

"And?" Darlene says.

"She's not in her cell. I start to freak. I'm like, Tad, you stupid son of—but then she appeared at the side door and—"

"From the outside?" Darlene says.

He frowns. "Yeah."

"She was outside the jail," I say, "coming back in?"

"Yeah. She said she couldn't sleep, so she went out to have a smoke to help calm her nerves before going back to bed."

"Did she have cigarettes and a light on her?" I ask. "Did she smell like she had been smoking?"

He frowns again. "Didn't register at the time, but no . . . neither. But remember, she was back inside. I wasn't thinking anything, but she's still in custody, whatta I care if she went out for a walk or a smoke or to gaze at the fuckin' stars?"

"So she went back into her cell and stayed in there the rest of the night?" Darlene asks.

"Yeah," he says. "I know she did because—"

"What is it?"

"Shit, man," he says. "Son of a—"

"You closed the cell door, didn't you?" I say. "She didn't have a problem with it when she came back in, did she?"

"Didn't even register," he says. "I didn't even think about it. I just closed the cell door and locked it and told her *goodnight*."

"It's a long shot," Darlene says.

Tad Barnes is gone. Evening is giving way to night, and the mosquitoes are coming out of the swamp. We've walked over to our cars and are going over what he said before we go. Anna and the girls are already in the car with the air conditioner running.

"I don't know," I say. "She had plenty of time to do it. All evening unsupervised."

"Yeah, but how did she get all the way to the campground?" she says. "That's a thirty-minute drive. One way."

"She had the time," I say. "No one I know is more resourceful."

"You really think she did it?"

"I really think she could've done it."

"Well, I agree in theory she could have, but . . . that's a far piece from actually doing it."

"She said she was going to," I say. "We now know she didn't just have the motive. She had the opportunity too."

"But did she have the means?" she asks. "Was she able to get to the park, do the deed, and get back without being seen?"

"Maybe somebody did see her," I say. "But didn't think anything of it at the time. Didn't know who she was or that she was supposed to be in jail."

"It's possible. Ol' Tad didn't know the significance of certain things until he saw them in a new context."

"We need to go back to the witnesses—especially Evelyn Hillman—and get a detailed description of every vehicle that pulled into the park that night," I say. "Then see if there were any down here that match the descriptions. See if anyone's car was stolen or if anything was out of place in it when they got back in after their shift at the jail."

"As I said, it's a long shot, but yeah, we need to check it out. Just to be sure."

And then it hits me.

"What is it?" she asks.

"Think about how many patrol cars are parked over by the jail," I say. "What if she took one of them? Nobody would mess with her. She could monitor dispatch and the other deputies the entire time. What if who Evelyn Hillman thought was Cody Faircloth doing his rounds was actually Randa Raffield there to kill Chris?"

44

That night as I am about to look at the other female victims found in parks around the state for similarities to Rebecca Blackburn, I glance at the phone log as I move it to the side.

I see the number that looks familiar to me again and wonder where I know it from.

It's frustrating that I can't remember, and I want to hit the table, but Anna and the girls are asleep.

Pushing my frustration to the side, for now, I dig back into the case files Captain Jack gave me.

But like before I can see no pattern, no similar victimology, no series these disparate woman can be a part of.

Leaving their physical descriptions and lifestyle details for the moment, I start examining their autopsy results, and that's when, randomly, unrelatedly, I realize why the unknown phone number on the log looks familiar to me.

I pick up the call log and look at it again.

The number is just one digit different than a number my brother, Jake, used to have. In fact, it's all the same numbers—it just has two of the digits transposed.

So I don't know the number at all. It just reminds me of Jake's old number.

This frustrates me even more than thinking I knew it but not being able to place it.

I stand to get some water and try to shake off the frustration and reset my mind, and that's when the image shakes loose in my mind and floats up to my consciousness.

It's an old snapshot of Jake sitting in an ancient Ford pickup he used to have. Over his shoulder, across the back window behind him, he has a gun rack, like nearly everyone in Pottersville did back then. The top two hooks hold a Browning 12 gauge with a beautiful woodgrain finish. The middle two hooks are empty. But the bottom two hooks hold an old-fashioned, narrow wooden Louisville Slugger bat like the blood-covered one found in the swamp not far from the blood trail where Chris had been beaten to death.

Jumping up, I quickly pen Anna a note and rush out the door into the night to look Jake in the eyes when I ask him about his bat.

"Figured you'd be by here long before now," Jake says when he opens the door.

"Oh, yeah? Why's that?"

"You know why."

"You gonna invite me in?" I say.

"Why don't we have a seat out here beneath the stars?"

He joins me on the little wooden porch in front of his single-wide, closing the door behind him.

"Have a seat," he says, gesturing toward one of the two wooden rocking chairs on either side of the whiskey barrel table.

We each ease down into a rocker and begin slowly rocking back and forth a bit.

I realize again just what a lonely little life Jake is living, and it makes me sad anew.

Since dad lost the election for sheriff of Potter County and Jake lost his job as deputy, he had mostly just floundered, working odd jobs, watching as the rest of the world seemed to keep moving—mostly away from him. I had married Anna and moved to Wewa. Dad now had Verna. Our lives were full and busy, but Jake had no one and not much to do.

I feel a pang of guilt that I haven't done more to try to help Jake and recommit to doing just that if I get the opportunity.

"Where's that skinny old Louisville Slugger you used to have?" I say.

"I'm gonna tell you what every criminal you've ever asked about something like this has told you," he says.

"It was stolen?" I say.

He smiles. "It was stolen."

"And I'm gonna ask you what every cop always asks next," I say.

"Did you fill out a police report?" he says. "Oldies but goodies."

"Why'd you do it?" I ask. "First, why'd you leave the bat out there?"

"Always best to leave the weapon behind," he says. "'Sides . . . figured you'd see it and know it was mine and might look out for me."

"Might?"

"You know what I mean," he says. "I wouldn't expect you to tamper with evidence or setup an innocent man or anything, but I thought you might not have too much heartburn with maybe sort of directing the investigation into who fucked up Anna's ex with a baseball bat away from your baby brother."

"Why'd you do it?" I ask.

"Needed to be done," he says. "Nothing else seemed to be working. He broke into your home and held your family hostage, John. Put a goddamn gun up to Johanna's little head."

"I know. I was there."

"If anyone ever needed a Louisville Slugger taken to them it was that bastard."

"Sure, but—"

"Remember that trouble I got into a while back with the search and rescue boys?" he says.

I nod.

"You saved my life in more ways than one," he says. "Kept me from gettin' fuckin' raped and kept me out of prison. Mom's gone. Nancy's in New York and not coming back. Dad's getting old and has his health issues. 'Fore long it'll just be the two of us. I knew you weren't gonna get physical with him—or that you wouldn't want to and you'd feel guilty as fuck if you did, so I . . . pinch hit for you."

"Jake . . ."

"I know we ain't close like some brothers are," he says. "But . . . you're. . . my big brother and . . . I . . . love . . ."

"I love you," I say. "And I . . . thank you for what you did."

"I wasn't the only one," he says. "Merrill beat the shit out of him too. And Dad had already gotten in a few good licks on his sorry ass earlier that day."

"How did—" I begin, but my phone starts vibrating.

I pull it out to see that Reggie is calling, which given the hour means I need to take it.

"Hey," I say.

"Where are you?" she asks, her voice stressed, breathless.

"Pottersville. What's up?"

"Cody Faircloth is holding Melissa and Channing Tate at gunpoint in their RV. How fast can you get to the campground?"

45

"I'm not a bad guy," Cody is saying.

"I know that," I say, though I know nothing of the sort.

I'm in the open doorway of Channing and Melissa Tate's RV, my hands up showing I don't have a weapon.

Cody is facing Melissa, pressing the barrel of his .40 caliber Glock into the side of her head, his own forehead leaning into hers. She is wearing a thin, pale yellow tank top and white cotton panties and nothing else. She has an end-of-summer tan, more beige and bronze, but all the color has drained from her face, and it appears anemic and clammy.

A few feet away Channing sits in his recliner, pressing his palms into the gunshot wound in his abdomen, his wife beater as red as his suspenders, the once-white fabric soaked through and dripping blood.

"I'm not crazy," Cody says. "I didn't imagine what we have."

"No," Melissa says, "you didn't. We have something so . . . unique."

I can't tell if she's being sincere or just saying what she thinks he wants her to.

"You're singing a different tune now that that old fat fuck

over there is gut shot, and I'm holding a gun to your head," he says.

Instead of Cody's eyes being wide and wild like I'd expect, they're actually sleepy hooded slits which I suspect means he's drunk or on some form of downer.

"I . . . You know I couldn't be honest before," she says. "Channing was standing right there."

"And now he's sitting right here."

Cody's hands are shaking, and though the air conditioner is running and the RV is frigid, he's sweating profusely.

"It's different now."

"Yeah," he says. "There's a .40 caliber Glock pressed against your temple."

Though the front of my body is cool, the back, with the door open out onto the summer night behind me, is hot, and I can feel beads of sweat trickling down my back.

"No, I mean I can be honest now," she says. "I am being honest. I love you. I want to be with you."

"Prove it," he says.

Channing's head is hanging down now, and he's emitting soft, low moaning sounds.

"You prove you're not a bad guy," I say, "by letting me get Channing some help before he bleeds out. Put the gun down."

"How can I prove it?" Melissa says to him when he doesn't respond to me.

"Tell me to finish him off and leave with me now," Cody says.

"I'll leave with you," she says. "Let's go. But there's no need to kill silly old Channing. You kill him, and they'll always be hunting us. Let him live, and we can be together. Let him live for us."

"You're just saying that 'cause you want him and not me," Cody says. "You want me to let him live so you can get back with him."

"That's not it, I swear," she says.

"Then prove it."

Cody seems so unhinged that I suspect he will fire his weapon whether he means to or not.

"I can't."

"Think about all I've done for you," she says. "What I've given up, what I've sacrificed, what I've done."

"Cody," I say, "prove you're not a bad guy. It's not too late. We can still fix this. But that gets a lot a more challenging if someone dies. Let me get the EMTs in here to help Channing."

"Look, *John Jordan*, all this is your fault anyway. Coming at me the way you have been. So why don't you just do everyone a favor and shut the fuck up."

"I thought you wanted a life with Melissa," I say. "A future."

"I've got no fuckin' life left. You saw to that. Now I'll just settle for no one else having a life with her."

"Even if that's true," I say. "Don't you want some more time with her first? You can buy more time with Channing. Let the EMTs come in and get him. You can keep me if you want, but let him go."

"Would you *please* shut the fuck up," he says.

"I thought you let me in here so I could help," I say. "That's all I want to do. Make it so everyone gets out of here alive—including you. You can have your life back. It's just a few good decisions."

"I swear to fuckin' Christ Almighty if you say another word I'm gonna shoot you in the fuckin' face just to get you to shut the fuck up."

Jake

H e would be dead or in prison right now if it weren't for John.

Instead, he's outside the Tate's RV at the Dead Lakes Campground with Reggie, the EMTs, and a few other Gulf County cops, while John tries to get the dumbass deputy to put his gun down and not kill anyone else.

John didn't hesitate when Reggie told him Cody would only talk to him and only inside the RV. No weapon. No vest. No hesitation.

He had always respected his older brother. Even when he didn't understand him, even when he was so jealous of him he couldn't see straight, he respected him. And that had only grown in the last few years. Now he liked him, loved him, and respected him.

Of course, he was gonna come to his defense. Of course, he was gonna help protect John and his family from the mental motherfucker tryin' to destroy them. There was never any question.

He'd always liked Anna and felt bad for her. He knew how humiliated she had been by Chris—as if it had anything to do with her, as if it was her fault somehow.

He saw firsthand the toll it had taken on both of them, John and Anna, and he had watched it long enough, stood by and done nothing far too long.

Besides, when you really thought about it, what did he have to lose?

When he asked himself that at the time, he thought, *Got no family—besides Dad and Verna, John and Anna and my two nieces —got no career, got no girlfriend, got nothing going on really and no damn prospects, so of course, it has to be me.*

He had to be the one to step up to the plate. It was when he had that thought he knew he had to take the bat to Chris.

He had beaten the fuck out of that sorry piece of shit who

had held a gun up to his little niece's head. He had enjoyed every second of it. He doesn't regret anything he did. He'd gladly do it all again.

C hanning only has moments—unless it's already too late —and Cody doesn't seem like he's going to put down his weapon voluntarily.

I'm close enough to tackle him, but there's no way he wouldn't be able to squeeze the trigger and open Melissa's skull before I even got a hand on him.

"We coulda been so happy together," Cody is saying to her.

"We still can, baby. We can. You gotta give us that chance."

I can't tell for sure, but I believe she's lying, just saying anything she can think of to try to keep Cody from killing her.

"You're such a practiced whore," he says. "You'll say anything right now—and hell, you're halfway believable."

"What do you have to lose?" she says. "If you're gonna kill us all anyway, what do you have to lose to see if I'm telling the truth? You could give us a try, you and me. You could always kill us later?"

He seems to think about that.

It's a good argument, and at first, it seems like he's convinced.

"I don't know ..." he says. "I don't know."

"Remember what you said to me the last time you were inside me," she says. "Remember that? What was the line from that poem? Don't tell me we don't ever get to feel that way again."

He shakes his head as if a bee is buzzing around it. "God-damn it, you're good. You're the damn devil. How could I have been so fuckin' stupid?"

He shoves her away, and she falls back over the table and onto the bench beside it.

As he does, he's no longer pointing the gun at her, so I dive in his direction.

He turns, bringing up the gun.

Quick. No hesitation. No thought. Just action.

At first, I think he's bringing the gun up to fire it at me, but quickly realize he intends to shoot himself.

Which he does. Without hesitation. Without flinching. One quick, fluid motion.

Under the chin. One shot. The back of his head exploding as I tackle him to the floor.

Melissa screams. Loudly. But it's barely perceptible against the ringing in my ears the discharge of the weapon in the small space has caused.

I roll off of Cody Faircloth as EMTs rush in to work on him, and I continue to lie there a moment as they realize there's absolutely nothing they can do for him and turn their attention to Channing Tate.

One of the EMTs says something to me. Reggie is at the door asking me questions. I have yet to move. And I can't hear either of them, which at the moment is just fine with me.

46

I crawl into bed beside Anna, head aching, ears ringing, exhausted, but wired.

She rolls over and backs up to me, and we spoon in the cool darkness, the soft sounds of the girls breathing and occasionally stirring coming through the baby monitor, the digitization of the noises transformed into something hollow and tinny.

I try to sleep. I need to sleep. Soon I find I am unable to sleep.

Every time I close my eyes I see Cody's head exploding.

When I'm not seeing that, I'm seeing Chris's head bashed in by a long, thin old-fashioned Louisville Slugger.

Of course, Chris's head wasn't bashed in. But that didn't prevent me from seeing it.

In my mind, I see Dad, Merrill, and Jake brutally beating Chris, see them and Anna and Reggie and Sylvia taking turns stabbing his dead body.

And then I realize the significance of the twelve stab wounds. Agatha Christie used twelve stab wounds for the victim, a Mr. Samuel Ratchett, in *Murder on the Orient Express* because twelve is the number of people on a jury.

Does it mean what I think it means? I'll have to give it some more thought, but right now I'm still in shock, too wound up and wired to think about it.

Eventually, I slip out of bed and pad down the hallway to the kitchen table and the copies of case files Captain Jack gave me.

Anna had punched holes in the papers and placed them in a binder for me. I pick up the binder and walk around the kitchen and living room looking at its contents.

The binder feels like a book in my hands, my actions of walking around with it and flipping through it reminding me of reading, and there is something comforting and inspiring about it.

I flip from victim to victim, searching for similarities, looking for patterns, trying to find Rebecca's killer hiding behind them.

But they're too different, too disparate in their ages, hair and eye colors, body types, races, and backgrounds.

Apart from being shot in a similar manner—execution style —and being buried in shallow graves in Florida state parks and campgrounds, I can see nothing that connects them.

And then I take a closer look.

I discard all the victims that were shot with a different caliber weapon, shot in another part of the body, or shot more than once.

I now have a much smaller group of mostly young female victims—ones that match Rebecca almost identically regarding manner of death and body disposal.

These are cold killings. Not the passionate murders of obsessed and jealous and mentally unstable boyfriends.

I look to their autopsy results for additional evidence, searching for signs of rape or torture.

There are none.

The killings just grew even colder.

These are executions like the ones often seen by contract killers.

It's rare to see young women so dispassionately dispatched from their lives.

Who is the iceman who's doing this?

You're a cold bastard, aren't you?

I then see two things almost simultaneously that together roll the fog back for me and give me a glimpse of this sociopathic serial killer.

All the young women on this more narrowly defined list were killed and buried in campgrounds like the Dead Lakes Recreational Center where Rebecca Blackburn was found. Not state parks. Not hiking trails. Not national parks. All were killed and buried in small, private or county-run campgrounds.

The second thing I see at nearly the same moment is all the young women's autopsies reveal scarring to the backside of the pubic ramus bone and changes in the uterine musculature and the breast tissues. Just like Rebecca.

"That's it," I say aloud.

"What's it?"

I spin around to see Anna squinting at me from the hallway.

"Did I wake you?"

"No. Well, maybe, but only by not being beside me. What's up? You couldn't sleep? You look like you're officiating a wedding or a funeral standing there with the binder like that. Though you usually don't do those in your underwear."

"You know I've never done a nudist wedding," I say. "It may be the only kind I've never done."

"What is *it*?" she asks.

"I think I've got it," I say. "Captain Jack was right. Sort of. There is a pattern. It just includes a much smaller group than he thinks."

"Tell me."

"All the victims like Rebecca had given birth recently," I say.

"Really?"

"And they were all killed and buried like Rebecca in smaller campground sites like the one here," I say. "Not state or national parks."

"In how big an area?" she asks.

"What do you mean?"

"How spread out are they?" she says. "The campgrounds where the young women were found?"

"All over the state."

"So it couldn't be Cody Faircloth," she says.

"Right."

"Then who?"

"That first day I saw Carla," I say. "I was so surprised to see her there at the crime scene. I asked her what she was doing there, and she lied and said she was there to see me. But I think she was there to try to sell her baby on the black market, and it was only after she saw me and we reconnected that she floated the idea of us adopting her child."

"Who was she there to see? Was Chris involved in some sort of black market baby adopting scheme?"

"When Evelyn Hillman first told me about Rebecca and her baby being in the park with her parents it sounded odd," I say. "The way she described it . . . they didn't sound like a family really. I don't think they were. I think they were meeting to do the adoption, to make the exchange. I think after she went back home and started trying to live her life again she got to missing her baby and decided she wanted him back, so she went back to the guy who arranged the adoption and demanded to get her baby back, to expose him if he wouldn't, and he killed her."

"Who? Captain Jack? Is that why he really goes to all these crime scenes all over the state—'Cause he causes them?"

"There was another older couple with a young girl and a baby at the park recently," I say. "They appeared and acted very similar to the way Rebecca and her family were described. And we know it wasn't her parents. They never came to the park. It was the couple adopting her baby—just like the ones I saw there recently were. I think HC Thompson is behind it all. He introduced the couple as his son and daughter-in-law, though the man looked nothing like him, and the young girl and her baby as his granddaughter and great-granddaughter, but I don't think they were. He only introduced them when Evelyn forced him to. I think they were there to adopt a black market baby. I think anytime there's a problem, or the girl wants her baby back or threatens to report him, he kills her."

"Is his wife involved or is it just him?"

"I have no idea," I say. "It's just a working theory, but if I'm right . . . she could be, or she might be involved in some part of it— the adoption part, but not the killing of the girls who come back and threaten to cause trouble. I just don't know. But . . . because he's a host and moves around from campground to campground to be a host, he's killed these young women all over the state. It'll be easy enough to see if he was the host at these other campgrounds. But we can start by asking Carla if she was there to see him that day."

47

"She's not answering," Anna says.

While I have been getting dressed and calling HC Thompson, Anna has been calling Carla.

"Neither is he," I say.

"Oh, John," she says.

"It's the middle of the night," I say. "They could be asleep, have their phones off. Could be all sorts of reasons they're not answering."

"Most people answer calls they get in the middle of the night," she says. "And Carla is supposed to be at Rudy's, just dozing with her phone right beside her on the counter."

"Have you spoken to her lately?" I ask.

"Not since you talked to her about us wanting her to tell the biological father," she says. "What if us saying that sent her right back to him?"

"This is just a theory. I could be wrong about all of it, but even if I'm not and even if what we said sent her back to him, she hasn't had the baby yet. He won't harm her until after she has the baby. And maybe not even then. I don't think he killed all the mothers—just the ones who threatened him or wanted their babies back."

"Still," she says. "I'm scared."

"It's going to be okay," I say, though I'm not convinced that it is.

"I'm gonna ride up to the campground and see if HC and Georgia are still there," I say.

"Why wouldn't they be?"

"They probably are," I say, "but with all the heat up there, they may have been planning to leave after this latest adoption, but then after what happened tonight with Cody and the Tates. . . They may have decided to take off tonight. I just want to check. I'm gonna call Reggie on the way up there. I want you to call the Potter County Sheriff's Department and ask them to send a deputy by Rudy's to check on Carla. If she's there, ask them to stay with her until I can get there. Call me when you know something."

I feel a certain relief and release of tension when I reach the Dead Lakes Campground and see HC and Georgia's camper is still here.

On the way up, I called Reggie and told her my theory. She's waiting to hear back from me once I confirm HC is still here.

One thing she said during our conversation still echoes through my mind, haunting me with a deep, dark sense of dread. *It struck me as odd that HC didn't come over and check on things at the Tates' at any time tonight.*

I pull over to the host camper, my eyes scanning the park as I do.

It's dark and quiet. No movement. No signs anyone else besides me is awake.

I pass by Channing and Melissa's RV, the door of which now has crime scene tape covering it.

When I reach the host camper, I jam the car into park, jump out, and rush over and start knocking on the door.

There's no answer.

I knock louder.

Still nothing.

I start to bang on the door.

There's no movement inside, no indication that anyone is home.

Eventually, I'm banging and yelling so loudly that Evelyn Hillman and Captain Jack appear at either side of the camper to see what's going on.

"Either of you seen HC or Georgia?" I ask.

"No, not lately," Evelyn says. "Why? What's wrong?"

"How long has it been since you've seen them?" I ask.

Jack shrugs. "Couple of days."

I look back at Evelyn. "Yeah, a day or two. What is it?"

"Either of you have a key to their place?"

"I do," Jack says.

"You mind getting it and let's go in and check on them?"

He pulls a large ring of keys out of his pocket and begins to flip through them as he walks over to the door.

I let him unlock and push open the door, but then I step around him and inside.

I call for them, but it's immediately obvious no one is here.

Even in the dim light, it's apparent the place is immaculate and mostly empty.

"Never seen the place so clean," Jack says from the doorway.

"Don't touch anything," I say.

"This ain't my first barbecue," he says, holding up his hands.

I search the place thoroughly but know before I do that I'm not going to find anyone here.

"Is their other camper still over there?" I ask, nodding in the direction of the field beyond which is the trail Chris was tortured and killed on.

He leans out the door and looks.

He's nodding when he leans back in the camper. "Sure is."

My phone rings. "John, she's not there," Anna says. "There's no sign of her. They woke up Rudy, and he has no idea where she is. Said she was supposed to be out there watching the diner. Is she up there? Are the Thompsons?"

"We're still looking," I say. "I'll call you back as soon as I know something."

"That *is* their truck out there, right?" I say.

Jack looks out and looks back in nodding. "Yep. That's theirs."

"Do they have another vehicle?"

"Pretty sure," he says. "Never seen it, but . . . HC's alluded to it."

"How close are y'all?" I ask.

"Not very," he says.

"But you have a key to his place?"

"Said he wanted me to have it in case he ever decided to pull the pin."

"Pull the pin?"

"Yeah. We used to talk about life off the grid. Disappearing if you needed to and never being seen again. Contingency plans. Survivalist stuff. Told me he had everything all setup and one day he was gonna pull the pin. Walk out of his life and never come back. Completely and utterly disappear. Said if he ever did while I was here, I could have the stuff he left behind if I'd do a few things for him."

"Like what?"

"Some paperwork I think. I'm not sure exactly. Said if he ever did it, he'd leave me some instructions. Do you think he did it?"

"Pull the pin?" I say. "Yeah, I think he did."

48

Howard Carter "HC" Thompson

Howard Carter "HC" Thompson was born in Raiford, Florida, the fourth of five children. His father was a raging alcoholic, his mother a stern disciplinarian. In his youth, he was an Eagle Scout and heavily involved in 4-H.

He ran away from home several times as a teenager and served a significant amount of time in juvenile detention centers. After high school, he enrolled in seminary but soon dropped out because of disciplinary issues.

For the next several years he worked odd jobs, took night classes, and was in and out of trouble with the legal system.

He was first arrested as an adult for embezzling $42,000 from a medical practice where he had secured a job as an X-ray technician using forged credentials. He was only sentenced to three years' probation.

Two years later HC was arrested again—this time for embezzling funds from the insurance agency he was working at, an action that only resulted in the extension of his probation.

Over the next few years, his probation was extended yet again after another arrest, this time on charges of securities fraud and mail fraud in connection with a phony medical consulting company he had formed in Sarasota.

After HC finally completed his probation, he was able to stay out of trouble for a couple of years, but shortly after that he was arrested again on multiple charges of embezzlement and fraud and check forgery. This time he was actually given jail time. He served 60 days in jail. After his release, he formed a bogus investment company and swindled $55,000 from a friend.

Over the course of the next two and a half years, he started two more fraudulent shell companies, and it was during this time he hired a pretty, young assistant named Gina Lippmann. Before long, Gina disappeared, and HC told her friends and family he had sent her away for training. But after not hearing from her again, her parents filed a missing persons report. Police questioned HC, who denied any knowledge of her whereabouts. But a few days after HC was questioned by the police, Gina's parents received a typewritten letter from Gina assuring them she was okay but saying she didn't want to see anyone. After this, the investigation ended, and Gina Lippmann has never been seen again.

After laying low for a year or so, HC began working at a shelter for unwed mothers in Orlando. And this is where his foray into black market adoption began.

During this time, HC placed a number of babies with wealthy couples who were unable to have a child of their own, and though he made a small fortune doing so, not only did none of the young mothers ever see a dime of their part of the money, but many of them went missing and were never seen again.

For more than a decade, HC moved his black market baby business from town to town just ahead of investigators— always with the same pattern, mothers not being paid or not being seen again.

As HC grew older and technology continued to advance, he began living further and further off the grid, more and more on the fringes of society, eventually marrying Georgia Cathy and becoming an itinerant host at campgrounds, as he continued to trade babies for large sums of money and as young women continued to go missing from the areas around the campgrounds.

49

W hen I get home, I find Anna asleep on the couch, the baby monitor and her phone on the coffee table next to her.

Her phone is vibrating.

When she doesn't stir, I pick it up and answer it, stepping into the kitchen and whispering, so I don't disturb her.

"Oh, John?"

"Yeah?"

"It's Audrey Taunton."

"Hi, Audrey. Are you okay?"

"I was returning Anna's call," she says. "She called my phone and Carla's looking for her. The poor dear is here. Just showed up tonight, said she didn't know where else to go. Wanted to let y'all know she's fine. Sleeping soundly."

"That's great news," I say. "Great news. Thank you so much for letting us know."

"Would have sooner but it was so late, but then when I saw Anna had called both of us, I knew it was okay to call."

"I need to speak to Carla," I say. "Could you wake her up for me?"

"Sure. Hold on just a minute."

Inside of forty-five seconds, Carla's sleepy voice is saying, "Hello."

"It's John."

"Hey, John."

"Are you okay?"

"Yeah, just . . . got a little overwhelmed. Needed to get away. Didn't know where to go, so I came to Grandma Audrey's. It was like . . . I don't know . . . I just sort of realized I was here."

"That's great. I'm glad you did. You're safe there. I just wish you would've felt you could've called us or come here."

"I did," she says. "I didn't not call y'all 'cause I didn't think I could. Nothing like that. I just . . . With the whole adoption thing . . . I just . . ."

"I understand," I say. "I need to ask you about that. It's very important."

"Okay?"

"That day I first saw you at the Dead Lakes Campground, at Chris's crime scene," I say, "why were you really there?"

She hesitates a moment, eventually saying, "To see a man about helping find a couple to adopt my baby."

"What man? What's his name?"

"Howard."

"Howard Carter Thompson?" I ask. "HC?"

"Yeah. Why?"

"Have you spoken to him since then?"

"I called his number when things didn't work out between us . . . but it was disconnected."

"Don't try to get in contact with him again," I say. "And if he tries you, don't answer. Don't engage with him in any way. Don't let him know where you are."

"Why? What is it?"

"We think he killed Rebecca Blackburn and—"

"Who?"

"The young woman in the swamp behind the camp-ground," I say. "And we think he's killed others. Some of the mothers he helped get their babies adopted."

"Oh my God," she says. "Really? That . . . could've been me."

"But it wasn't. We're gonna find him. Everything's going to be okay. Just get a good night's sleep and call us in the morning."

"Could y'all come pick me up tomorrow?" she asks. "My old car finally died, and even though she's trying to get me to go ahead and take it, I just can't accept Grandma Audrey's car. Not and . . . I just can't."

"Sure. We'll be happy to. See you then. Get some rest. Love you. Night."

I say it the way I say it to my daughters, and it feels just as natural.

"Love you," she says. "Night."

"Who do you love?" Anna asks.

I turn to see her standing in the case opening between the living room and kitchen.

"Carla," I say. "It was Carla. She's okay."

"She is? Oh, thank you, God. Where is she?"

I tell her.

"Oh, John, that makes me so happy. Yes. Thank God. *Thank you, God*. Isn't it just the best possible news?"

It is. There's no doubt about it. But, as is too often the case in this life, it is followed the next morning by the worst possible news.

50

The next morning, a beautiful, breezy day in September with low humidity and plenty of sunshine, Dad, Merrill, and Jake are arrested.

When I open my eyes and look up, Anna is standing there.

Trying to blink away the fog I say, "Huh?"

"Reggie's on the phone for you."

I grab my phone off the nightstand to discover it is dead. I thought I had plugged it in, but evidently, I was so exhausted and out of it, I failed to do it.

"On my phone," Anna says. "Here."

She hands me her phone as I sit up and try to sound awake.

"I've been calling your phone," Reggie says. "So has Darlene."

"Sorry. Guess I forgot to plug it in before I fell asleep this morning. What's up?"

"Tony Ford has arrested your dad, Jake, and Merrill Monroe."

"What?"

"Darlene swears she was just as blindsided as the rest of

us," she says. "They're sitting in our jail awaiting first appearance, and then he's gonna try to move them."

"I'm on my way."

"The hell you playin' at?" I ask Tony Ford when I walk into Reggie's office.

"No hard feelings," he says. "Nothing personal. I'm just doing my job. Same as you. I follow the evidence where it leads."

"What evidence? There is no evidence."

"I've kept things back," he says. "Had to. There was no way you guys were ever gonna let this be a legit investigation."

"That's exactly what we're running," Reggie says, "and I resent the implication that we aren't. I invited you in to assist us. That's all you were supposed to do—assist us with our investigation."

"I know, but when I saw how close you two were and where the evidence was leading . . . I knew the only way to do this was on my own. Had to keep things from Investigator Weatherly too. I know she was feeding you information. And that alone should let you know I'm only doing what I had to, what you would do if you were in my position."

"It'd be one thing if you suspected me or John of corruption," Reggie says. "If you felt like you had to arrest us—I mean, hell, that's what FDLE does—but to make arrests in our case without knowledge . . ."

"There was no other way," he says. "And if you think about it honestly you'll know it's true."

"The only thing that's true is that you have the wrong men in custody," I say.

"My supervisor and I disagree," he says. "I have his support. I didn't go off halfcocked and do this. I conducted an investigation, gathered evidence, built a case. I'm sorry you don't like it. I knew you wouldn't. And, hell, I don't blame you, but . . . I have investigative integrity, and if you two are what you're claiming to be, you'll appreciate that, respect it, even if you don't like it."

"It's so obvious what you're doing," I say, "but it's not going to work."

"Oh yeah? What am I doing that's so obvious to everyone but me?"

"There's no way you think they all three did it," I say. "You're hoping one of them will take a deal and turn state's evidence on the others, but there's no way that'll happen."

"See? Right there. That shows how much you know. Because it already has."

A fter Tony Ford is gone and Reggie and I are alone, she says, "I know you want to get over to the jail to talk to them, but I wanted to give you an update on . . . We've setup roadblocks and put out BOLOs for HC and Georgia Thompson, but so far . . . nothing."

I nod.

"Do you think she was involved in it with him?" she asks.

I nod. "*How* involved is the question," I say. "She went along with the lies about the people there for adoption being their family, so she was involved in the black market adoption scheme. What I *don't* know is if she knew about or was involved in the murders. I hope we get the chance to ask them."

"One more thing," she says. "Cody wasn't the father of Rebecca Blackburn's baby. Neither was the coach. A fellow student was. Cody was a mess and involved in all sorts of immoral and illegal shit, but lately, he was mostly just obsessed with Melissa Tate. Oh, and it seems Channing and Melissa weren't swingers so much as Melissa was a pros and Channing was her pimp."

"Makes more sense," I say. "He gonna make it?"

"Still in surgery."

I nod slowly and am about to leave.

"The media and members of the public are saying that Cody Faircloth's actions and those of your dad, brother, and best friend, show a pattern of corruption in our department and they're calling for the governor to replace me and for FDLE to do a full investigation of our agency."

"I'm sorry, Reggie," I say. "I—"

"Always knew this was a temporary gig," she says, "but I didn't want to go out in disgrace and under indictment. Of course . . . If I'm being honest . . . I probably deserve it . . . It's karma for that other thing."

That other thing is what her mother did, which, if there's an investigation into our department, will most likely come out too.

51

"Would've been here sooner," I say to Dad when he comes into the small interview room of the Gulf County jail. "Just found out."

He shakes his head and waves off my explanation. "Doesn't matter," he says. "Nothing you can do."

It's disconcerting to see this lifelong law enforcement officer and the superhero of my childhood wearing a bright orange jail jumpsuit.

The inmate attire and the general unkempt state of him make Dad look older and smaller somehow. His gone coarse gray hair is standing up wirily in spots, his eyes are bloodshot, dark puffy bags beneath them. He has white stubble on the loose skin of his cheeks and neck, and the wrinkles on his face and forehead look more like the deep ridges and crevices of permanent furrow than the benign lines of time.

"The FDLE agent has been running his own little parallel investigation," I say. "Keeping us out of it."

He nods. "It's what we all figured he'd do."

"We didn't figure on him making arrests, bringing charges, taking over the case like this."

"It was always a possibility," he says. "And given the circum-stances . . . pretty . . . inevitable."

He seems so resigned I can feel my own resolve receding a bit.

"Reggie feels terrible for asking FDLE for assistance," I say. "Says she wouldn't have if she had known this was how it would go."

He shakes his head. "She made the best decision she could at the time. Nobody blames her. How's your brother holding up?"

"I haven't seen him yet," I say. "Merrill either. Wanted to talk to you first . . . because of something Ford said."

He smiles and nods. "I knew there was no way he'd be able to keep it to himself."

Ford had hoped at least one of the three would turn on the other two. What he hadn't counted on was one of the three turning on himself *for* the other two.

"So it's true?"

"In some ways . . . looking back . . . it seems . . . It was always gonna come to this."

"It doesn't have to," I say. "I just need a little more time. Let me . . . Give me a chance to see what I can do."

"To be honest I'm afraid of what you would find," he says. "This way it's settled. It's over."

"But it means you're going to confess to a murder you didn't commit," I say.

He shrugs.

I shake my head. "Dad, after decades as a highly respected sheriff . . . all you're going to be remembered for is confessing to killing your son's wife's ex-husband," I say. "It's not right."

"The older I get, the less I care what others think," he says. "And I damn sure won't care how I'm remembered once I'm in the ground."

"I care," I say.

"I know you do, and I'm sorry about that, I really am, but . . . would you rather it be your brother or your best friend?"

I don't say anything.

I think about the ongoing investigation into Chris's dealings as an attorney, into his firm and partners, into the fraud and extortion and corruption. I frantically try to think of a way to use it to get Dad and Jake and Merrill out of here but know there's nothing in it that can save them—and even if there were, it will most likely be years before the investigation is concluded.

"They're young men," he says. "Have a lot of life left in them. Me, I'm old and sick and . . . not gonna be around much longer anyway."

Something inside me sinks at the thought of a life without this man in it, even in the background somewhere mostly out of sight. I'm not ready to lose him. And I'm certainly not willing to let him go out like this.

"I don't—"

"I feel like I've failed Jake," he says. "I want to give him another chance at a decent life. This is a way for me to do that. Let me do it for my son. It's nothing you wouldn't do for your daughter. But he's gonna need your help to have a better life. Will you help him? For me? Will you make it so what I'm doing is . . . worth it? That it actually works."

"I'll do anything I can for Jake," I say. "Of course I'll help him, but let me see if I can help you too. I'm sure there's a way out of this for all three of you."

He shakes his head. "There's not. I've run every scenario through my head. And even if by some miracle you were able to get them off of me, Jake, and Merrill, it would just put them on to Anna or you. That's no better. This way . . . By me doing it this way . . . it's the best possible outcome for all of us."

I shake my head again. "I just can't . . . accept that. There's got to be something I can do."

"There isn't," he says. "Not without manufacturing evidence or playing defense attorney games. This way . . . is best for everybody. And I'm happy to do it. More than happy to do this for my children and grandchildren. I would've been happy to kill Chris, and I did beat the hell out of him at his house earlier in the day, so it's not like I'm innocent. Just think about how gladly you'd do something like this for Johanna. Especially if you knew you didn't have long to live anyway."

"I just can't . . ."

"You can't solve every mystery, Son. Can't close every case. Accept the limitations of what you can do. It's a valuable, valuable lesson."

The Serenity prayer echoes through my mind, but I don't want to accept the things I cannot change. I don't want to let my dad do what he's about to. I don't want to admit that I can't fix this, figure out a different outcome.

"These last few years with Verna have been some of the happiest of my life," he says. "So . . . completely . . . unexpected. So . . . In so many ways . . . perfect. I've felt like a young man again. You gave all that to me. All of it was a gift from you."

I feel tears stinging my eyes, and I look away and blink several times.

"I wouldn't've had that if you hadn't done what you did for Verna and me in Janet's case. You not only gave me Verna back, but you gave me Nancy back too. You do so much for so many all the time . . . I don't think you realize just how much. But . . . you've got to let others do things too. I still feel so guilty about how I acted when you moved to Atlanta after school. It's one of the greatest shames of my life. Let me do this for Jake and Merrill and . . . for you and Anna and my granddaughters."

I don't say anything. I can't think of anything to say.

"Letting me do this for y'all will be harder than all the

things you do for all of us all the time," he says. "It's easier to do things for others than to let someone do something for you—especially for someone like you. But you can. You're strong enough to let me do this for Jake, for you. I know you are."

"I'm not sure I am."

"You are," he says. "I know you are."

52

Before I can see Jake or Merrill, they are taken to court for first appearance.

For now there is nothing to do but wait.

After hearing Jake, Merrill, and Dad plead not guilty and have their bail set, Verna, Zaire, and I meet briefly about making arrangements to get them bonded out.

I wasn't surprised to hear dad enter a plea of not guilty. I knew his plan was to plead not guilty at the hearing and to make the plea deal with the state's attorney's office later—a deal that would see the charges against Jake and Merrill dropped for Dad's full confession.

While Verna and Zaire work on taking care of the bonds, Reggie and I meet with Darlene in Reggie's office.

"I tried to call you this morning as soon as I knew," Darlene says. "I didn't know a thing until it was happening. Clearly, he didn't trust me."

"Do you have any idea what he has or thinks he does?" I ask.

"Not really, no," she says. "I overheard him saying something about your father's prints at Chris's house and Jake's prints on the bat this morning, but . . . I just caught bits and pieces if it. He was trying to prevent me from hearing any of it."

"Anything else?" Reggie asks. "Can you think of anything else?"

She shakes her head. "Sorry, I just . . . I don't think I know anything you don't. But . . . I did hear him say all the lab results were back. Have y'all seen those?"

"No," Reggie says, "we haven't."

"There must be something in them he's using," I say. "Something he doesn't want us to see."

"Oh, we're gonna see them," Reggie says. "It involves the Rebecca Blackburn labs too. That's your case. And both cases are under my jurisdiction. You can bet your sweet ass we're gonna see them."

She snatches up her phone and calls Jessica Young and instructs her to get copies of the lab results from FDLE and to let her know if anyone gives her any trouble in getting them.

"I'm so sorry for all this," Darlene says. "I . . . If I had known I would've told y'all."

"Which is why you didn't know," Reggie says. "He knew."

"The thing is . . . if I thought the evidence pointed at your dad or brother or Merrill or anyone, I would have told you," Darlene says. "I wouldn't go behind your back or plan some sneak attack on you. The evidence is the evidence. If it's there, you have to go with it, but you don't have to be sneaky or under-handed about it. I haven't seen enough of the evidence to know who is or isn't guilty, but I'll help y'all in any way I morally and ethically can."

"We wouldn't ask you to do anything immoral or unethi-cal," Reggie says.

W hile we're waiting for Dad and Jake and Merrill to
bond out and for Jessica to get us copies of the lab
results, and for any reports from the BOLOs on HC and
Georgia Thompson, I meet Anna and the girls and Carla for
lunch at the Sand Dollar Cafe. They have just returned from
picking up Carla in Tallahassee.

"Sorry again that I gave y'all such a scare," Carla says.

Having made our selections from the cafeteria-style serving
line, we are seated at the back table in the small dining room,
Taylor in a highchair at the end of the table between Anna and
me, Johanna sitting across from Carla, watching her
worshipfully.

"H ow did you scare them?" Johanna asks.
"It was just a misunderstanding," I say. "We didn't
know where she was and we were worried about her.
That's all."

"Oh. The way you would be about me if you didn't know
where I was, Daddy?"

"Exactly," I say. "Exactly like that. Carla is like a daughter to
us too."

"Then that makes you my big sister," Johanna says.

Carla smiles as tears fill her eyes. "Yes, it does. It absolutely
does."

"You, me, and Taylor Beth," Johanna says. "Best sisters."

"Best sisters," Taylor repeats.

"I should've told you guys," Carla says. "I didn't know I was
going until I did and then I thought I'd just get away for the
night and come back the next day. Didn't know where else to
go. I figured she was probably as lonely as I was and she's been
so nice to me."

"I'm glad you went there," Anna says. "It did her a lot of good too."

"I'm just so glad HC didn't answer when I called," Carla says. "Wonder why he didn't."

"He was too busy walking out of his life," I say.

"And y'all have no idea where he is?"

"None."

"He won't come after me, will he?"

I shake my head. "No, he has no reason to. He only does that which benefits him. Every action he takes is selfish and in the service of self-preservation. He'll stay as far away from us as he can."

"Good."

"Yeah, good," Johanna says. "But . . . even if a bad man did come around to try to get us . . . Daddy would protect us, wouldn't you, Daddy?"

"I would," I say. "And so would Anna and your mom and your granddad and Uncle Merrill and Uncle Jake and Reggie and an entire army of people."

"And y'all would protect Taylor Beth and Carla that same way, right?"

"Right."

Later, while Johanna and Taylor have walked back into the cafeteria area to get dessert, Carla says, "I see what you mean about Susan keeping Johanna from you all those years. You're right about it not being fair to my . . . to . . . I've decided to tell him. He won't want anything to do with the baby and will be more than happy for you to adopt him if you still want to, but at least it will be his decision. I won't rob him of that."

"Really?" Anna says, her voice and countenance rising. "Are you sure?"

"I am. Are y'all?"

"We are," Anna and I say simultaneously.

53

When I get back to Reggie's office, her mother, Sylvia, is waiting for me.

"Mom has something she wants to say to you," Reggie says. "And she wants to say it to you in private, so I'll go see how Jessica is coming with getting those lab results from FDLE while you two talk. Oh, but before I forget . . . Channing Tate is out of surgery and in stable condition."

She closes the door behind her as she leaves.

"You've been avoiding me," she says.

I smile.

"I can't blame you. I know what a terrible position I've put you in. Reggie too, for that matter."

I don't say anything.

More slight than Reggie and without the river clay skin tone, Sylvia has the same blue-green-gray eyes—though sickness and time have caused them to fade and become partially obscured by drooping eyelids.

"And I'm sorry to force myself on you now," she says, "but I figured when you heard what I had to say you wouldn't mind. Because I'm the solution to your problem."

"What problem is that?" I ask.

"Two problems actually," she says. "The first is your problem with me—specifically me getting away with murder. Now, if I could confess and it not ruin Reggie's life, I would. I'd take this burden off her and you. But I can't. If I confess to what I did, not only will everyone know what Robin and the others did to her in high school, but they'll know she covered up what I did. Well, not covered up, just . . . didn't do anything about it once she found out. So I can't confess to what I did without destroying her life, and I'm not going to do that. But I could . . . and this will solve your second problem . . . I could confess to killing Chris. That way I would get punished for my crimes without making my daughter pay the price, and your dad will be released."

Before I came to work here as an investigator with the Gulf County Sheriff's Department, Sylvia had killed a group of men who had raped Reggie when she was in high school. When I arrived, the case was one of a few open, unsolveds I began to look into. Not long back, when Reggie and I were under sniper fire out near the swamp where Remington James had died, after getting shot and not being sure she was going to make it, she told me what her mom did and asked me to keep her secret. In the intensity of that battlefield moment and because I thought she was about to die, I told her I would—something I have regretted ever since.

"Thank you for the offer," I say. "It means a lot. I really appreciate you making it. But even if I were willing to let you try, which I'm not, it wouldn't work. Tony Ford and Darlene and others would see it for the false confession it is. There's no evidence."

"But I was there at the park the night he was killed," she says. "Reggie and I rode through the campground. I'm sure someone saw us."

"That's not nearly enough," I say. "Plus that would implicate Reggie."

"I could say I went back after Reggie dropped me off," she says. "That I saw him there when we rode through and went back and killed him later."

"I appreciate you being willing, but . . . it wouldn't work. Thank you, though. It means more than you can know that you offered."

54

"I ain't lettin' the sheriff take the fall for me," Merrill says.

Though Dad is no longer a sheriff, Merrill, like a lot of people from Potter County, still refer to him as such. He was, after all, the only sheriff many of us knew for all but the last few years of our lives.

"He's not," I say.

Because Zaire was called into emergency surgery at Sacred Heart, I picked up Merrill once he bonded out, and am now driving him back to his house in Pottersville.

"How you figure?" he asks.

"'Cause you didn't kill Chris."

"I beat the hell of out him," Merrill says.

"Sure, but long after that Jake went to work on him with a baseball bat."

Based on the evidence—the timing and partial bruising and healing of some of Chris's wounds—and some of what Dad, Jake, Merrill, and Anna have said, I am fairly confident Dad had a physical confrontation with Chris at his house earlier in the day, then Merrill beat him up on the trail on the backside of the field when he found him stalking Anna and the girls at the

Dead Lakes Campground later that evening, and then later that night Jake went to the same spot with a baseball bat and worked Chris over some more.

"Who's to say the blunt force trauma he suffered from my fists aren't the ones that killed him?" he says, adding as he holds up his fists, "You don't think these are far more devastatin' than a little Louisville Slugger?"

I laugh. "No, I'm certainly not sayin' that."

"So . . . he doin' it for Jake," he says.

"He's doing it for both of y'all," I say. "He said so to me when I spoke to him about it."

He nods. "I realize it's mostly for Jake, but even if a little is for me . . . I can't let him do it."

"It'll take blunt force trauma for you to stop him," I say.

"All I got to do is tell 'em I did it."

I shake my head. "They've already made the deal with him. They're not interested in you or Jake. You know how it is when cops get a narrative. They stick with it. They've got a former sheriff. Someone close to us. His arrest will do the most damage to the department, cause the most pain and embarrassment to our family. They know what they're doing."

"You sayin' I confess they'll just ignore it?"

I nod.

"Then I'll tell the media," he says. "Let's see them get a conviction then."

"It's a confession plea deal," I say. "There won't be a jury trial."

"But a judge has to sign off on it, right? Won't do that when a black man's on TV confessing to killin' a white man. This is still the Deep South."

I shrug. "It might work. Or it might get you both indicted. But he wants to do this—for you, for Jake, for me, for all of us. He wants us to accept this—this gift he's giving us—and go on with our lives."

"Well, I'm not so sure I can do that," he says. "What about you?"

"I'm sure," I say, "that I can't."

"So . . . what we gonna do?"

I shrug. "That's the problem," I say. "I'm far less sure about that."

55

W hen I get home, Jake is waiting for me.
He's sitting in one of the outdoor metal chairs beneath the pergola at the side entrance of our house.

"Come in," I say.

He shakes his head. "Nah. I just . . . You mind sittin' out here with me for a minute?"

"Not at all," I say, sitting in another chair next to him.

"Any sign of that murderin' HC asshole yet?" he asks.

I shake my head. "None," I say. "He has completely and utterly vanished."

He doesn't respond and doesn't say anything for a long moment.

"You okay?" I ask. "Sure you don't want to come in?"

"I'm sick of my own life," he says. "Tired of bein' such a fuckup. Even when I try to do somethin' good for someone . . . it gets all fucked up. I try to make things better . . . and I just make 'em worse."

"You mean Chris?"

"I's just tryin' to help," he says. "Saw what he was doin' to you and your family. Knew he needed to be dealt with. Knew you wouldn't do it—I mean, you know, like with a bat. Wanted to step up and do my part . . . for our family. I don't have anything goin' on. No career. No girl. No . . . nothin'. So . . . I got time on my hands . . . why not take care of the Chris problem? And look at the fuckin' mess I've made."

"I know why you did what you did," I say, "and I appreciate you doing it for us."

"But as usual I fucked it up," he says. "And now Dad's gonna spend the rest of his life in prison."

He pauses, but I can tell there is more, so I wait.

"Thing is . . ." he says. "I can't let that happen. I have to do somethin'. But I'm scared if I do, if I try to, all I'll do is fuck things up worse. 'Cause . . . that's what I do. So . . . I'm askin' for your help. Help me get Dad out. Tell me what to do. How to do it. I'll gladly take his place."

I nod. "I'm working on it. I'll let you know what we can— Actually, you can start by answering a few questions for me."

"Sure. Anything."

"Do you think you killed Chris?"

He nods. "Had to have. Didn't mean to. Just meant to hurt him. Teach him a lesson. Bust him up some so he'd leave y'all alone."

"Exactly," I say. "And he was alive when you tossed the bat into the swamp and left."

"I thought he was."

"And you didn't break into the camper in the field and get things to stage the crime with, did you? You didn't put a hood over his head and stab his dead body twelve times and drag it over and prop it up at the picnic table, did you?"

"No. I just left."

I nod.

"You sayin' I didn't kill him?"

"If you did, why would someone come along and do all

those other things I just mentioned, plus steal a phone and call dispatch and report it?"

He shrugs. "I don't know. Why?"

"Because—"

My phone vibrates, and I pull it out of my pocket and glance at it.

I t's a text from Reggie saying she finally got the lab results and final autopsies from FDLE and that she has just emailed them to me.

"Hold on a second," I say to Jake and call Reggie.

"Hey," she says. "Get my text?"

"Have you read the reports yet?" I ask.

"Yeah. Glanced over them. Why?"

"Any surprises?"

"Chris's cause of death," she says. "It wasn't blunt force trauma from the beating he took, and it wasn't the stabs after he was already dead."

"What was it?"

"Asphyxia," she says. "He died from asphyxia as a result of an overdose of OxyContin."

"Thanks," I say, as Anna appears at the door.

"Who killed him?" she asks.

"Someone he'd trust enough to take pain medication from."

"What is it?" Anna says as she opens the door. "What's wrong?"

56

"I know you killed Chris," I say.

"*Me?*" she says, her voice rising.

"Yeah. He called you for help. He was in excruciating pain. He had been beaten up three different times that day. He was a user. He called you when he needed something. So he called you. He called you, and you came. And you brought the pain meds you had left over from your surgeries."

I am sitting in the interview room in the investigative unit of the Gulf County Sheriff's Department, pictures of Chris and copies of his autopsy and lab results and crime scene photos splayed out on the table in front of me.

Across the table from me, having been read her Miranda rights and being recorded on audio and video, is Chris Taunton's murderer, his mother, Audrey Taunton.

"I don't know if you brought them with you with the intention of killing him or just to help with this pain, but you brought them, and you did kill him with them."

She doesn't say anything.

"I had to ask myself why were there all these calls to you that night—you and your husband—and then they just stopped. They stopped because you told him you'd come help him. Then a while later, time enough for you to drive over to help him, there was one final call from you. That was the call once you had arrived to see exactly where he was, wasn't it?"

Her lips twitch, but she still doesn't say anything.

Apart from the lip twitch, she appears completely calm, an old lady in her own little world, sitting on a bench at a department store waiting for her daughter and granddaughters to finish shopping—or something like that.

"You get there, and you see what kind of shape he's in, and you ask him what happened and what he's doing here, and somehow it comes out that he was beaten up by Anna's family and friends. And maybe you say something like *let's call the police*, but he says *no. Don't call the police*. Why? Because he was there stalking Anna and our girls. And Anna had just told him the damage he paid a madman to inflict on her had actually caused developmental delays in his own daughter. He didn't want anyone to know what he had done, what he was still doing. He just wanted you to help him, give him something for the pain and get him home."

I lift a picture of Chris, the one in his best suit before his world began to unravel, and say, "Your own son—"

"Was a weak, using, obsessive, stalking, manipulative, murdering . . . who wasn't going to stop. He was going to keep on harassing Anna and my granddaughter until he killed them or someone stopped him."

"So you stopped him."

"I did what any responsible mother would do. I stopped him myself. He was in pain, so I said, 'Here, take these. They'll help. And when they take effect, I'll help you home.' And he said, 'Isn't that too many, Mom?' And I said, 'No, dear. It's just some mild pain pills and an anti-inflammatory.' And he took them."

"Of course he took them," I say. "Just like he did when he was a sick child and his mother was caring for him."

"He wasn't going to stop on his own. He had to be stopped. It was the most humane way to stop him. I just . . . helped his pain go away, just helped him go to sleep."

A sleep he would never wake up from, I think.

"He cut me out of his life," she says, her small, moist, hooded eyes locking onto mine. "Acted like I was dead for decades. He killed that young girl he was having an affair with, Ashley. Tried to kill you. Almost killed Anna and my granddaughter. I knew what he was capable of. What I did for him was far more merciful than anything he ever did for anyone else. He never did anything decent for anyone—not that didn't benefit him in some way."

I can't imagine getting to a place so dark, being in a situation so hopeless, that I could think my best or only course of action would be to kill my own child.

Johanna and Taylor's sweet, smiling faces flash in my mind, and I know with absolute certaintyI am incapable of ever getting to such a place. No matter what. It's unfathomable. Unthinkable.

I feel bad for Audrey.

To have a son like Chris, to live with the knowledge of who he was and what he was doing for so long, knowing he wouldn't stop, knowing the damage he was inflicting, then arriving at the desperate moment of utter despair where she became convinced that death by her hands was better than the half-life he was living.

"I don't think it was premeditated," I say. "And I'll tell you why. Breaking into the camper, getting the things you did so you could stage the scene. Shows you didn't bring anything to use except the pills themselves, which you can argue you brought just to help with his pain."

"I don't care," she says.

"About?"

"Whether anyone thinks it was premeditated or not. I don't care if I get a long sentence or a short one. Either way, it will be a life sentence *and* either way my life won't be any different than it is now. I live in a one-room cell as it is. Have no life. Failed at the only job I ever had—being a mother."

"Why did you break into the camper?" I ask. "Why'd you put the hood on him, stab his body, move it over to the picnic table?"

"I didn't," she says. "I didn't stab him. I couldn't . . . do . . . something . . . like . . . that."

"You didn't stab him with a Swiss army knife after he was already dead?" I ask.

She looks as confused as she does alarmed. "*No. Gracious me no.* Was he . . . Did someone do that to him?"

"Let's just stick with what you did for right now," I say. "Then we can talk about anything else you like. Okay?"

She nods slowly. "Okay. I . . . I covered his head with the pillowcase because . . . and I . . . I couldn't leave him out there in the swamp to rot. And I couldn't stand to see his face after I . . . after he was . . . So I covered his head. I moved him so he'd be found sooner. I covered his head to . . . hide his face."

"Did you have help moving the body?" I ask.

She shakes her head. "I needed it. It's why I didn't move him very far."

"Where did you move him to?"

She looks confused again. "Where you found him, I'm sure. I dragged him out of the swamp to the . . . to where the trail begins. Just at the backside of the field where that empty camper was. I'm not as frail or weak as I appear—or have pretended to be since Chris's death. It wasn't easy. It took me a while. But I was determined. I rested a lot. And . . . well . . . in certain circumstances we are capable of far more than most of us think—even old ladies who've had their knees replaced."

So she hadn't been the one to stab him or move his body over to the picnic pavilion.

"Then I drove back home," she says. "On the way, I called Lyle and told him he needed to go check on Chris, where he nor anyone else would think I had."

I nod and try to think of anything else I need to ask her. "Is there anything else you'd like to say?"

She nods. "Just that I'm sorry. I'm sorry for all the damage Chris did. I'm sorry to the families of all his victims. I'm sorry to Anna and Taylor and Johanna and you. I didn't raise him to do the things he did. And for myself . . . I'm sorry to your father and brother and friend for letting them be arrested for something I did. I wanted to say something. I did. I picked up the phone so many times to call and confess, but each time . . . found I was weaker than I thought I was. And in that, and to my shame, I reminded myself of my son."

57

"I think I know why you staged the crime scene and body the way you did," I say. "But I'd like to hear it from you."

"Am I supposed to know what you're talking about?" she asks, though it's obvious she does.

I'm in an interview room at the Liberty County jail with Randa Raffield because I don't want her back inside the lax Gulf County jail even for a brief visit. She had already escaped once and she now had leverage over Patch McMyers, the correctional officer who let her do it. I didn't want to risk bringing her back there again. So I came to her.

She's wearing a white inmate jumpsuit with large black stripes, yet still has the appearance of someone to be reckoned with.

"We've made an arrest in the case," I say. "We have a confession. I'm not looking to jam you up or add any charges to you. Just seeking answers, searching for confirmation."

"Who'd you arrest?" she asks. "Who confessed?"

"The same person you saw trying to drag the body off the trail and into the field," I say.

"You've got to give me a name if you want me to talk," she says.

"Chris's mom," I say. "Audrey."

"Poor weak old thing," she says.

"You saw her struggling to move the body so it'd be discovered sooner," I say.

"I saw her making a mess of things," she says. "Decided to clean up a little after her. After all, she had just done what I had come there to do."

"How'd you know he was going to be there?"

She shakes her head. "I'm not gonna tell you that and you don't want me to."

"Did you take one of the patrol cars from the side of the sheriff's office?"

She smiles. "Ironic, isn't it? Gave me a good laugh all the way there and back."

"So tell me about this cleanup job you did."

"She had a pillowcase over his head, which I get . . . but by adding a cinch around his neck, it made it look more like the hood of the condemned than someone close to the victim covering his face."

"Yes it did."

"Figured might be a good idea to get him farther away from the trail," she says. "Thought sitting him up at the picnic table like he was just hanging out was a nice touch."

I nod. "It was."

She shrugs. "Then I just thought . . . This needs something else. So I . . . I stabbed his dead body to make it look like something other than what it was."

"I noticed you stabbed him twelve times," I say. "Was that inspired by *Murder on the Orient Express*?"

She laughs. "Jail library is for shit, but they've got a few Agatha Christies. Just reread it and . . . I don't know, I guess it was fresh on my mind. And I thought so many people wanted Chris dead . . . What if I made it look like a group did it—like a jury. So I made different kinds of stabs—short and shallow, long and deep—but . . . It might have worked if I could've done it while he was still alive, but I just couldn't. Got there a little late for that.

"His mom took his phone—probably thought she was getting rid of evidence of their calls or something, but she left a lot, so I got rid of the rest of his personal things. I didn't do as much as I would have liked. Figured she was going to call to report it so he'd be found sooner, plus I needed to get back."

"Why?" I ask

"Why what?"

"Why break back into jail when you were free?"

She smiles. "Because, John, I told you. I'm gonna beat the charges against me. I went back because I know I'm going to win. Lot easier to be ruled innocent than live a life on the run."

"It was good of you to do what you did for her," I say. "I mean what you tried to do."

"I'm a good person," she says. "I keep telling you."

"You were going to kill Chris," I say.

"I told you I would," she says. "And I keep my word. He needed killing. It was the good thing to do. I was doing it for you, John. I knew you weren't going to do it. And if it wasn't done sooner or later, he was going to hurt or kill someone close to you."

I don't respond.

"If Anna or Merrill or your dad or Daniel had done it, you wouldn't stop thinking they were good people," she says. "I don't deserve any less consideration."

"No, I guess you don't," I say. "I guess you don't."

"I'll tell you something else good I'm going to do," she says.

"What's that?"

"Well, two things, actually," she says. "I'm gonna look out

for Audrey while we're in here. Take good care of her. Just like she's my own grandmother."

I know she means it, and I'm glad she's going to. And it's not because Lyle Taunton has threatened to kill her—he's just out of his mind with pain and blame and grief, and wouldn't kill her even if she was a free woman in the outside world—but because jail is going to be difficult for Audrey, and taking care of her will be good for Randa too.

"And when I get out of here," she continues, "when I have all these silly legal battles behind me . . . I'm gonna help you solve crimes and catch bad guys. Something I'm utterly and uniquely qualified to do. We're gonna make a great team, John. A hell of a team."

58

"She had an accessory," Anna says.

I nod. "Yes she did."

It's later that night. The girls are in bed. Anna and I are on our back patio beneath the stars, looking at the shimmering reflection of the full moon on the still surface of the glass-like lake.

We are seated beside each other in metal-framed canvas chairs, holding hands, the baby monitor, her wineglass, and my empty Diet Dr. Pepper bottle on the rough cement floor between our chairs.

The warm night is quiet and peaceful, relaxing and restorative.

"Even when I began to suspect her," I say, "I had a hard time believing she could move the body to where we found it, prop it up the way she did, and stab it. I should've known sooner that she had help."

"Actually, she had two," she says.

"Two?" I ask. "Helpers?"

"Two accessories," she says. "One before the fact and one after the fact."

Thinking I know where she's going with this, I shake my head. "Just one," I say. "*After* the fact."

"You're talking to a lawyer, John," she says. "I may not be practicing at the moment, but . . . I know . . . things. An accessory *before* the fact is someone who counsels or instigates another to commit a crime. An accessory *after* the fact is someone who, having knowledge that a crime has been committed, aids, or attempts to aid, the criminal to escape apprehension."

"Right," I say, "and in this case, there was only—"

"Randa was an accessory after the fact," she says. "She tried to aid Audrey from being apprehended, but I . . . I'm also guilty. I'm an accessory before the fact. I instigated others to . . . harm and ultimately kill Chris. None of this would've happened if it weren't for me. I called him. I taunted him. I told him where we were going. I put Merrill in the position he was in—up there watching us, knowing Chris was going to show up. I set this whole thing into motion. I'm far more guilty than Randa is."

I nod. "I understand what you're saying, and I know how you feel. But you're not responsible for Chris's death. You didn't make Merrill beat him up. Dad or Jake either. You didn't force Audrey to give him an overdose. And you didn't cause Randa to break out of jail and stage the crime scene—something she only did because she was too late to kill him herself. Something you couldn't have stopped. That's not on you. None of it."

"I'm not saying I'm as guilty as the person who pulled the trigger," she says. "I'm saying I loaded the gun."

"I know what you're saying and—"

"I'm not sayin' I feel bad about it," she says. "I'm just acknowledging my part in it. I'm confessing to my confessor that I know and take responsibility for what I did."

"You called Chris," I say. "Yes. You confronted him about what he had done and what it is costing his daughter. And you told him where you'd be—even taunted him. But you didn't make him come up there any more than you made Merrill work him over or Jake take batting practice with him, or his own mother, who had her own issues with him, to murder him. You didn't. I know what you did. And you didn't load the gun. You didn't instigate anyone to commit murder. You're not an accessory before the fact from a legal or morally responsible way. Wanting him to die, wanting him to attack you so you or someone else could put him down, is not the same as doing it. You're an amazing, force-of-nature woman. You're a fierce and faithful mother and wife. You are not an accessory in the murder of Chris Taunton."

"But—"

"It'd be far easier to make the argument I'm guilty of insufficient action in protecting my family than you are guilty of actions you took," I say. "But if it's okay with you I'd really like it if we didn't make either argument. Chris isn't worth it."

"You won't get any argument out of me about that," she says.

"So it's a deal?" I ask.

"All I wanted was to acknowledge my actions, take responsibility for them, and get your absolution," she says.

"You've got it—even though you have no need for it," I say. "And I'm asking for yours right back. I can't help but feel like I should've never let it get to this, that I should have been the one to . . ."

"You kept our family safe in every sense of the word," she says. "And you gave Chris opportunity after opportunity to repent and take advantage of the second chance he had been given. You couldn't have done things any differently and been you and I wouldn't have you be anything other than what you are, John Jordan."

59

On a warm, bright, clear late September Sunday afternoon, our friends and family gather with us in our backyard for a cookout.

Our honored guests are Dad, Jake, and Merrill, whose legal troubles are far behind them. But everyone seems to feel happy and honored to be here.

It seems as though everyone has put aside all worries and concerns so we can enjoy the day and each other. Anna and I aren't thinking about developmental delays or the state of the world we brought our daughters into. No one appears to be thinking about HC and Georgia Thompson not being found yet —or if they ever will be—or if and how we're going to find all the babies they adopted out over the years and what we're going to do with them when we do, or anything else related to work or the world outside of the world of our backyard.

So far Captain Jack, and therefore the internet, doesn't know about HC or the young women he killed, and very few people know about what Audrey did. Neither will remain that way, but for now, we are being left alone to enjoy our day.

Randa, who is in need of a mother figure, is looking out for Audrey while they are in jail together.

Chris is dead. Our friends and family didn't kill him. His dad, Lyle, has dropped his lawsuits, and no assault charges are being filed against Dad, Jake, and Merrill.

It's the weekend, so we have Johanna, which makes me even happier, and she and Taylor are playing with Tater who is chained in the far corner of the yard so he won't constantly jump on our guests, which he would if he were free. Our guests include Dad and Verna, Merrill and Zaire, Jake, Reggie, Merrick, Sylvia and Rain, Sam and Daniel, Darlene, Anna's parents, Jessica Young and a plus one none of us have ever met before, Carla, and a few other coworkers and friends from our community.

Those invited but not present are Michelle McMillan, who is still angry with me because Tommy was moved to another institution—even though I had petitioned successfully for it to be Calhoun CI, which is less than a thirty minute drive for her —and Tony Ford, who has acted like a petulant child since his case unraveled. It's just as well they didn't come because everyone here today is happy.

Perhaps nobody is happier or more relieved than my Anna. No longer living under the constant threat and continuous harassment Chris brought to her and her family, she is radiant with relief, buoyed up by hope and happiness, her calm countenance that of a content and fulfilled woman whose family is safe and secure and well.

"Are you as happy as you look?" I ask.

She has come to the grill where I'm preparing my world famous juicy Lucy cheeseburgers with an empty tray for me to refill.

"Happier," she says and kisses me. "Never knew such happiness existed."

We both know enough to know it won't last, that life, even a life as fine and blessed as ours, is an ebb and flow, the incoming and outgoing tide of which brings happiness and heartbreak, ecstatic pain and excruciating joy. But we both also know enough to be present and mindful and grateful for every moment like this one when we are together, surrounded by our most loved ones, in the serenity and beauty of a North Florida fall afternoon.

Later, I find myself down by the lake with Merrill, Jake, and Dad.

Julia is as calm and peaceful as she ever gets. Beyond the smooth surface of her face, the evening sun backlights the cypresses and pines rimming the far side with a deep, bright pink-orange glow.

"I want to thank each of you for what you did for my family and me," I say. "What you did and what you were willing to do."

"Think it's clear who was willing to do the most," Merrill says, turning toward Jake. "Ol' Slugger here went to bat for his family, didn't he?"

"He did, indeed," Dad says.

Jake tries not to show how much they mean, but it's obvious tour words make him stand a little taller, smile a little broader.

"But," I say, "next time y'all decide to play a hand like that . . . deal me in from the beginning."

They nod.

"Will do," Dad says.

"Hell, it ain't like we knew what each other was doing," Merrill says. "Couldn't exactly call any of us master planners, could you?"

"I don't know," I say. "Jake planned enough to bring a bat."

Merrill is about to say something when Anna rushes up and says, "Carla's water just broke. We've got to get her to the hospital."

I immediately start moving in the direction of Carla and the car.

"We'll take care of everything here," Dad yells after us.

"Let us know if you have any problems with anyone at the hospital," Merrill says. "We'll send Jake with his bat to take care of it."

I make no comment on how worried Anna appears or remark on how it's too early for Carla to give birth, I just react, just join Anna in doing what needs to be done in this moment without knowing if what comes next is one of life's ebbs or flows, an indescribable joy or a devastating pain.

I react to Anna's words, but I do my best not to react to the grimace on Carla's face or troubling words that "Something's not right."

"It's gonna be," Anna says. "We'll see to that. Don't worry. Just relax. Everything's going to be okay."

Her saying so is enough for me and seems to be enough for Carla.

A newfound calm and confidence seem to wash over us as Anna and I get on either side of Carla and help her toward the car.

Soon enough we'll know if our belief in Anna's words, which seem to be backed by the peace and beauty of the day, are justified, but for now all we can do is put one foot in front of the other and stride toward what is next, what is on the other, unknown, side of right now.

As we do, I whisper a prayer for Carla and her baby, our baby, asking for favor for what is to come, expressing trust and appreciation no matter what that might be.

ALSO BY MICHAEL LISTER

Blood Stone

Blood Trail

(Jimmy Riley Novels)

The Girl Who Said Goodbye

The Girl in the Grave

The Girl at the End of the Long Dark Night

The Girl Who Cried Blood Tears

The Girl Who Blew Up the World

In a Spider's Web (short story)

The Big Book of Noir

(Merrick McKnight / Reggie Summers Novels)

Thunder Beach

A Certain Retribution

Blood Oath

Blood Shot

(Remington James Novels)

Double Exposure

(includes intro by Michael Connelly)

Separation Anxiety

Blood Shot

(Sam Michaels / Daniel Davis Novels)

Burnt Offerings

Blood Oath

Cold Blood

Blood Shot

(Love Stories)

Carrie's Gift

(Short Story Collections)

North Florida Noir

Florida Heat Wave

Delta Blues

Another Quiet Night in Desperation

(The Meaning Series)

Meaning Every Moment

The Meaning of Life in Movies

Sign up for Michael's newsletter by clicking here or going to
www.MichaelLister.com and receive a free book.

CPSIA information can be obtained
at www.ICGtesting.com
Printed in the USA
LVHW091539030519
616572LV00002B/349/P

9 781947 606104